BLOOD IN
THE ASHES

Addelyn Davis

Bierds Publishing, LLC

To all the men (and especially women) in red and blue. We see you. And we salute you.

CONTENTS

The young woman cowered in fear as the thud of heavy footsteps echoed one by one on the concrete steps above. Her arms ached from the ropes that secured them behind her, the thick restraints biting deep into her slender wrists. She could taste the salt in her tears as they soaked into the bandana that silenced her. The footsteps continued at a slow, taunting pace, and as they fell closer, she squirmed backwards with each step. A mixture of blood and sweat streamed down her forehead, the knot at her temple throbbing with her every move.

Shutting her eyes, she thought of her parents, her friends, and wondered if they had even noticed that she was missing. Everyone had been so drunk at the party, especially herself, as she had never so much as tasted a wine cooler before that night. It was her first week in the new sorority and she had been too nervous to turn down an invite to the end of rush party so she had gone along and then some. She never imagined that she would learn her lesson this way. How long had she been down here? Her mother would be devastated when she found out what happened to her baby girl. She wished her mother was here now, that she would wake her up in her own warm bed and comfort her, letting her know that all of this was just some terrible nightmare.

Darkness fell over her body as she realized in terror that the footsteps had stopped. She continued to squeeze her eyes tight as she turned her face towards the damp floor in a feeble attempt to hide from her abductor's sinister gaze. She heard him chuckle as he took in her battered form and she held her breath as he leaned towards her. He reached down and grasped her arms, hauling her to her feet, her body shaking as he twisted her around. She tried to thrash and scream through her gag and restraints but even adrenaline could not subdue the alcohol slowing her motor functions down and she did little more than aggravate him with her resistance.

The man tugged her by her bound arms and dragged her across the room; her feet stumbled as she was pulled backwards, the sweat stinging her eyes and making it impossible for her to see. He brutally swung her around and threw her onto an old mattress that had been tossed in the center of the room.

She winced and coward, and fearful of his intentions on that mattress, jutted out a leg and heard a satisfied thud as her heel connected with bone. Before she could even register a gleam of satisfaction that she had hurt the man, fist connected with her temple and everything began to go dark. As the room faded from view and the stars danced around her vision, she swore she heard the flick of a lighter, then everything went dark.

CHAPTER 1

Olivia groaned and flipped onto her stomach, slapping the pillow down over her head. The sound of raindrops smacking the glass of her bedroom window filtered through the soft vise and she squeezed it tightly over her ears to block out the sound.

Please don't let it be a thunderstorm, she groaned. This was the seventh storm in two weeks and she started her shift in less than an hour. Olivia kept her eyes shut as she tried to drift off into sleep. With a mutinous roar, a resounding *boom* rattled her bedroom as a flash of lightning peeked through the confines of her pillow.

"Yuck!" Olivia shouted in defeat as she tossed the pillow to the ground and sat up in her bed, the sheets tangled around her legs. The whole Austin population had been thrilled with the storm systems that had ended their two month dry spell, but she and her fellow firefighters dreaded the fire-inducing lightning that ultimately came along with it. *Job security* was what her fire chief had called it.

"Job security my ass," Olivia grumbled as

she climbed out of bed and stalked into the bathroom, the wood floor creaking under her bare feet. She flipped on the light and grimaced at her tangled mass of hair as she grabbed her toothbrush and spread a small amount of paste on the bristles.

Chief Wesley Turner, the bane of her existence at Fire Station 61, had expressed his disdain for Olivia ever since she had walked into his office three years ago. Since then it seemed as though his ultimate goal in life was to make every day of hers a living hell.

As she vigorously brushed her teeth she scoffed at the nickname "Chief" Turner had given her that day...'Runt'. Not only was that a stab at her stature, a mere 5'6" which was dwarfed by the over 6"0' average of the male heights at the station, but it was also an indication of the Chief's bitterness towards her nepotism. Considering his ex-wife had cheated on him and then taken almost everything he had, it certainly did not help the fact that she was a woman.

Andrew Miles, Olivia's father, had been one of the best in his twenty plus years as fire chief of Station 61. He had hung up his hat four years before and was spending a lot of his current time fishing with Darcy Wallers, a sweet redhead that had been a schoolmate of her father's in his high school years. Olivia had once heard that her husband had succumbed to lung cancer a decade before and Darcy had inherited and now owned the *Corner Bar* downtown that Olivia and the other firefighters frequented when not on shift. She had noticed her father making more frequent trips to the bar and she was thrilled when she discovered that rather than grooming a hidden alcohol addiction he and Darcy had actually been falling in love.

Olivia spit into the sink and washed the foamy paste down the drain. She wiped her mouth on a washcloth and chucked it into the laundry basket next to the tub. Thinking of her father gave her a renewed sense of determination and she clenched the sides of the sink as she turned back to the mirror.

"I earned that spot damn it," she countered aloud to her reflection after sensing a small amount of self-doubt creeping in. Sure she had connections, but she had to pass the same written and physical tests that the other firefighters had and she had done it all without complaining. She had done the stair climb, she had carried the hose through the obstacle course, and thanks to her upbringing she knew her way around the fire house and equipment. Not to mention the fact that Olivia had to endure the endless taunts from the male fire-fighters to be as she dragged and hefted what she liked to call the bane of her existence, a training dummy that weighed 165 pounds and was supposed to simulate a real person. Maybe she had looked silly at times, thirty pounds lighter than the mannequin and struggling as she tried to drag the offending creature to safety, but she had still completed the task like everyone else.

After a quick shower to tamper down the anger that threatened to rise in her, Olivia pulled her damp, dark hair into a ponytail and added a touch of mascara to the lashes that framed her golden-brown eyes. She slicked some chap stick onto her lips with one hand as she tugged on a pair of panties and her sports bra with the other. She grabbed her rainy day outfit out of her closet: a fitted black t-shirt, track pants, sneakers and a black windbreaker rain jacket.

After quickly dressing, she pulled the hood of the rain jacket up and tucked her ponytail into the back. Zipping her cell phone into her jacket pocket she headed to the kitchen and downed a glass of water. She grabbed a bagel out of the bag she had left out on the counter the morning before, a can of tuna and her keys, then dashed out the door and down the stairs into the downpour that was currently threatening to flood the lawn of her apartment complex.

As she reached the bottom landing she stopped and set the open tuna can on the floor underneath the stairwell and out of the rain. The cat that Olivia knew had been watching her from the bushes approached her tentatively and only when she stepped a few feet away did he begin chowing down on his treat, all the while never taking his eyes off of her. Olivia smiled and shook her head at the unfriendly stray, then headed towards the parking lot.

She unlocked the door of her beloved truck, a gift from her father when she had turned sixteen. It was a Ford F-150, black with leather interior, and Olivia was determined to hold onto it as long as she could. Not only was it reliable and functional, but there were so many memories she had driving that truck. Trips to the lake with her father, driving down Callaway Avenue to meet him for dinner after a late class, and seeing him smile at her from the passenger seat when he had taught her how to drive and she had successfully parallel parked for the first time.

She started the engine and headed towards the fire station, driving cautiously through the rising waters of the roadways. As she headed towards downtown, as always she could not help but admire and appreciate the view of the Capitol and surrounding buildings as they lit up against a backdrop of a dark sky with intermittent purple streaks of lightning. It was her favorite building in Austin because it was always in the backdrop of some of her best memories of growing up in the area. She made sure to keep an eye out for any stranded motorists or even the occasional homeless person who had not found a sufficient shelter from the flooding roadways or the bolts of lightning that seemed to be nearing as she drove.

Olivia turned her truck onto Johnson Avenue and parked behind the fire station then jogged into the cover of the garage, pulling her hood down and shaking out the wet strands that had escaped the elastic of her ponytail. She ran her fingers along her father's on the far right wall as she passed. He had saved six kids from a burning van when she was only a kid and the city had awarded him that small token in return. This was her morning ritual and she knew it was superstitious, but she always felt that in some way it would give her luck and keep her safe on her shifts.

"'Sup Miles?" Olivia ducked out of the way as her fellow firefighter and long-time friend, Nate zipped past her and headed toward the lockers, deliberately shaking his wet hair at her as he did. She watched in annoyance as he headed straight for the locker marked "Freeman" and shook her head when he shrugged out of his jacket and proceeded to soak the floor with water. She followed suit, careful not to slide on the tile, and opened the adjacent locker as she unzipped her own jacket.

Nate had been at Station 61 for seven years and he had always been a huge fan of her father's. They had grown up together in the same neighborhood and while they never hung out as much once they both had reached the awful peer pressure filled years of middle and high school, she still had fond memories of the boy who used to keep her company at the neighborhood pool on the days her dad was on shift. He had been a rookie fireman under Chief Miles and she had run into him once or twice while on her visits from college. He also had been less than thrilled when then-lieutenant Turner had been promoted to Chief. Unfortunately, tenure was a big thing in their line of work and Chief Turner had nineteen years as a firefighter, not all with Station 61, but still enough to earn him the top spot at the station. He had a reputation for being a hard-ass, but as much as Olivia hated to admit it, and boy did she hate to admit it, he had loads of experience in the field, and he was good at what he did.

When Olivia had joined Station 61 three years before, Nate had mentored her like an older brother would, aiding her in the day-to-day job at the station and occasionally sticking his nose out for her when Chief Turner was on the war path. She looked up to him and admired the intensity and drive she always saw in his sharp green eyes every time he battled a fire. It was as if he was up against the devil himself and she knew that fighting fires was more than a job to him, it was his life. Sometimes she felt as if he thought he owed it to her father to make sure that nothing happened to her.

"I thought you were supposed to be on yesterday?" Olivia questioned as she hung her jacket up in her locker and tossed the last bite of her now-soggy bagel into her mouth. She grabbed a towel from the top shelf of her locker and with a pointed look at Nate, bent down and mopped up his mess as she chewed.

He shrugged in response, shoving his rain slicker into his locker as well, "Scott asked me to switch with him for personal reasons, but now I'm getting the impression that I was duped into working a storm shift while he spends a nice warm day rolling around in the sack with his latest fling."

Olivia rolled her eyes in mutual agreement as she threw the damp towel back into her locker and shut the door. She headed over to the weight room in the back corner of the station, stepping quickly past the closed door of Chief Turner's office. Fortunately for her it was shut, but she heard his voice coming from the other side, a muffled mixture of fingernails on a chalkboard and disdain.

The weight room was more of a "corner" than a room, a space set aside with weight benches, a few running machines and a punching bag for the firefighters to keep in shape while they were waiting on their next call. Olivia loved the treadmill best as it was a way to relieve stress that came with working with Chief Turner. She hopped on and started jogging at an easy pace as Nate high-fived Lieutenant Sullivan who was lifting weights in front of the television on the wall. She watched as he went into a deadlift with a heavy set of dumbbells with perfect form.

The television screen was in the middle of blasting a weather image of red and dark green and Olivia grimaced as she picked up her running pace. She glanced around the firehouse and waved to

Dylan Rider and Scott Hamilton, who were ending their 24 hour shift and dragging out the door. As if on cue, Matt Brown and Erik Stalle ran in from the rain outside and proceeded to head into the kitchen for coffee, fist bumping the earlier crew guys as they switched shifts. She rolled her eyes as she watched them both shrug out of their wet jackets and shake them out onto the tile floor, just as Nate had done earlier. On the plus side, she thought with an inner chuckle, maybe Chief Turner would slip on the puddles and perk up her day a bit.

Dylan was your stereotypical fireman, with bulging biceps, cropped hair and a chiseled face to match his form. He was in his early thirties and had been with Station 61 for almost ten years, and not once had she seen him without his signature bronze mustache. He had been married once, but had recently gotten divorced, his wife not being able to handle the odd hours that her firefighter husband had to commit to. Olivia had met her a few times, and the woman was all ice and had rubbed all of them the wrong way. Needless to say, a lot of the guys at the station had encouraged him and even voiced their approval at his announcement of divorce the year before. Hell, they even held an informal celebration at the bar the day the paperwork was final.

Scott Hamilton was a rookie, like her, but newer as he had only been at the station for a year. Unlike Olivia, however, he seemed to be one of the Chief's favorites and Turner loved to exploit Scott's achievements and hold him up as his "golden child." She knew it wasn't Scott's fault, and it was hard to be mad at someone who looked no older than a teenager, with chestnut curls and wide brown eyes. He always reminded Olivia of a frightened deer, and she noticed he was more timid than most when it came time to fighting fires. The other guys had taken secret bets as to how many years he would last before he quit and right now the maximum bet was five years.

To be fair, a lot of rookies went through that stage, as Olivia was only three years into her career and she had just recently encountered those emotional doubts. This wasn't a job you could just "mess up" at. Any little screw up could jeopardize your life or others and that was somewhat of an adjustment for all new firefighters. Olivia had made plenty of mistakes herself, especially at the beginning, and fortunately for her the mistakes hadn't put anyone in danger. They had however continually caused the red on her ledger under Chief Turner to grow.

Matt and Erik had both been at Station 61 for about 4 years and both men were blonde, built and walked around with a strut that seemed to attract the busty women that hovered around the station and at the same time annoy their fellow firefighters. They had been college roommates and had been fortunate enough to both get jobs at the same station. This was pretty lucky considering the amount of fire stations in the Austin area, but not surprising considering that after her father had retired and Chief Turner took over, Station 61 had quite a bit of turnover. It seemed as though a couple of new attractive young women, "Fire Hoes" as Nate liked to call them, would flounce into the station every time those boys were just coming off their shifts.

She turned her attention to Lieutenant Dale Sullivan, who was currently spotting Nate on the weight bench as he maneuvered a heavy chest press. He was older than everyone at the Station but he still had the physique of a young man and that seemed to help him keep up with the rest of the crew, or as he fondly referred to them all as his "young 'uns". His face was lined with age and gray hair dusted his sideburns but he bench pressed like nobody's business. Sullivan was married with two kids and had been a part of Station 61 for 12 years. He was a burly man and Olivia always thought of him as a big soft teddy bear. Sullivan was always kind and his wife, Jenny frequently brought cookies and pies to the firehouse for the staff. His kids, Tommy and Jean were 8 and 6 respectively and the group always enjoyed having them come around to try on the oversized gear or honk the horn on the fire engine. He had even been offered the position of Chief before Turner had come around, but a family man through and through he decided to forgo the extra responsibility for his kids.

The lieutenant had worked for a long time with her father and both of them had been very good friends. She remembered her dad talking about the fishing trips they would take together on their days off and Olivia had attended many a family barbecue at the Sullivan house with her father while in high school. Sullivan had been there for her dad during her parents' divorce and if it was not for him, she knew her dad would have moped around a lot longer than he did after the split. She appreciated the lieutenant for that and looked up to him as a sort of father figure herself.

Olivia was suddenly snapped out of her thoughts and she whipped her head around as the station alarm started clanging. As she clambered off the machine and the firefighters all ran to their respective lockers, Chief Turner stomped out of his office, his face already formed into his trademark scowl.

"Alright *men*," he shouted, as he glowered at Olivia, "We've got a live one...two story house over on Lark Lane, get a move on it!"

Olivia sucked in a retort as she quickly hustled into her gear. The big coat and pants had been tailored for a woman but she still never got used to how heavy she felt once she was in full gear. In fact, the first time she had put on all of her gear she could have sworn that someone had sewn in the weight of the training dummy as a cruel joke. After yanking on her boots she strapped the breathing apparatus onto her back and around her waist and buckled it tight. She knotted her ponytail into a low bun and jammed the helmet down over her head, tightening the chin strap.

Her adrenaline pumped as she and the other firefighters jumped into the red truck and headed out of Station 61, tearing quickly onto Johnson Avenue, sirens blaring. She had been to her fair share of fires but the hasty panicked feeling that she got every time the siren on their truck sounded never left her. She glanced over at Nate to see that he was watching her intently. His gaze softened as he noticed her looking and he grinned and gave her a thumbs up. She bravely smiled nervously in response. Nate knew that while Olivia was no longer considered a "rookie", she was still fairly young in the game and he knew that she worried about the risks of the job.

She smelled the smoke three blocks before they even reached the blaze, and inhaled sharply as they came upon a large historical home that had flames lapping out of both stories. People were gathered on the sidewalk, watching or taking cell phone pictures of the blaze or just milling about to take in the action.

The chief barked at them to turn on their microphones and strap on their breathing devices and Olivia complied, slipping on her mask and clicking on the regulator. She followed Nate and the other guys as they filed out of the truck. The lieutenant and Erik headed over to the nearby hydrant to set up the hose, hustling bystanders away as they passed.

"Alright *Runt!*" The chief's voice slashed through her helmet and she winced at the tone, "I want you to sweep the upstairs and Freeman, you take the bottom floor. The rest of you help me out here with water and crowd control."

"Yes sir," Olivia and Nate responded simultaneously as they jogged towards the inferno. It frustrated her that the chief tended to really harp on her while they were on a job, but she knew that focus was the number one priority so she kept her retort to herself. Fighting fires were the only times Olivia let him get away with taking jabs at her without so much as an eye roll or glare in return.

Nate motioned for her to enter through the open front door as the blaze seemed to be situated on one particular side of the house at the moment and they both headed into the heat filled home. He nodded at the wooden staircase just in front of the landing and quickly turned to check out the ground floor while Olivia swiftly began traipsing up the steps.

Please stay on that side, she internally coaxed to the flames that were currently gravitating only to the east side of the house. She knew she needed to be quick and efficient before the fire blocked her only exit back down the stairs.

She headed towards the few bedrooms on the west side of the building, careful to avoid the flames that lapped at her gear on the opposite side.

She felt the heat of the fire seeping through her coat and pants and quickly scanned each room, checking closets and under beds and calling out to anyone who might still be trapped somewhere inside.

As she neared the back of the house the smoke thickened and she turned into what looked like a little girl's bedroom. She knelt down and quickly glanced under the bed as well as looked behind the little dresser and opened the closet, sweeping her arms through the stuffed animals and clothes that adorned the floor to make sure no one was underneath the stack.

Just as she had straightened up and finished her sweep of the room, a noise startled her and she whipped around, glimpsing a hazy shadow darting in the hallway past the bedroom door.

"Hey!" she called out through her mask as she scurried out the door and turned towards the direction she had seen the figure going. She peered down the smoky hallway as she looked for the person that had rushed past her. Olivia glanced down the empty wooden staircase, and grimaced as she noticed the flames edging closer to her one way out.

"Hello?" She called out again as she struggled to see through the thickening smoke. She groped down the walls of the hallway as her vision became more obscured, following the path to the only other room on the upper floor that hadn't yet been infiltrated by fire. She could almost hear the roar of the flames as they consumed the house board by board.

"Miles, you done with your sweep?" Nate's voice flooded her ears in a crackle of static.

"No Nate, I think I saw someone up here, I'm in pursuit," she replied.

"Freeman!" Chief Turner's voice crackled through, "You all finished in there, we need to get going before this fire jumps to another house."

"Done down here Sir!"

"Get out here quick Freeman, the fire's reached the front, you'll need to go out back. Miles are you finished upstairs?"

Olivia ignored the Chief in her haste and glanced around the final bedroom quickly. Her blurred vision swept over the cleanly made bed, the small white dresser in the corner and finally settled on the closet door in the back corner. She noticed that it was slightly ajar so she began to quickly jog towards it. Just as she reached for the knob, she stopped in her tracks as a crash sounded out down the hall she had just entered the room from.

Olivia turned and dashed out of the room, scooting along the wall to the little girl's room she had been in earlier, certain the sound had come from that direction. The fire had overtaken the upper landing of the staircase but she knew she would never be able to live with herself if she left someone up there to perish in the flames. Perhaps someone had been frightened of the growing fire near the landing and had retreated back to the corner of the house in panic.

"Hello?!" she called out into the darkened room as she felt her way through the gray hazy space. She made her way past the bed and threw open the closet door then peeked under the bed again, squinting into the smoke, but found no one. Frantically, she strained to listen for any signs that someone was hiding somewhere but she couldn't hear over the commotion outside and the crackling of the fire and charring of wooden beams that echoed throughout the house.

"Miles!" She could hear the Chief and Nate yelling at her as she ran to the closed window on the back wall of the bedroom and peered out into the hazy darkness. As she looked she thought she saw a tall dark figure running through the rain and into the woods behind the house. She squinted harder but the figure was gone, and swirls of thick smoke danced before her eyes causing her to question if she had even seen someone beyond the glass or if the smoke was playing tricks on her.

Olivia turned to face the bedroom door and saw that the flames from the hall had now wrapped themselves around the doorway and blocked her only exit. She whipped back around and gripped the underside of the window frame but to her horror, found that it seemed to be sealed shut as she lifted with all of her strength. Thinking quickly, she grabbed a small stool from the foot of the bed and heaved it towards the glass, feeling the shatter of the window reverberate through her arms as the wooden stool broke through the pane. She tossed the stool aside and felt her feet crunch on top of the glass as she approached the window. She hoisted herself up to the small opening but her gear prevented her from getting through by herself.

Hopping back down she frantically cried out into the microphone, "Nate, I'm stuck in the back bedroom; I can't get through the window with this gear on and the fire's blocking the door!"

Iridescent blue and orange flames danced across the wooden floor as Olivia tried again to hoist herself through the small window to no avail. There was no response from her helmet and as a split second decision she quickly unstrapped the tank and yanked the mask off of her face. She squinted as her eyes burned with the sting of arid smoke and her lungs burned as she coughed and sputtered while she blindly reached for the window again. She hoisted herself up just as the smoke began to overtake her and swung her body out of the window, gripping the broken pane with her gloved hands. She could feel the shards of glass puncturing through the material to get to her skin but she knew she would end up with more injuries than that if she fell.

Through watering eyes and hands burning under her weight she clung to the jagged edge of the window, her legs dangling precariously towards the ground. The dense smoke billowed out of the broken window as the heat of the nearing flames seared through her gloves.

"Let go!"

Olivia struggled to turn her head towards the voice that sounded out to her below but her position allowed for little movement unless she drop two stories to the ground below. The weight of what was left of her gear prevented her from seeing beneath her and she gripped the window pane in panic.

"Miles, let go!" She recognized Nate's voice shouting loudly through the roar of the fire, "Trust me!"

Olivia shut her eyes and released her grip, her stomach fluttering as she zipped towards the ground and landed in a pair of strong, solid arms. She coughed and wheezed as Nate gently flipped her over off of him and sat her up on the wet grass, yelling for oxygen. Large, wet raindrops smacked against her face and rinsed away the charred ash that covered her now-exposed cheeks and forehead.

An oxygen mask was swiftly placed over her nose and mouth as she was lifted and carried to the edge of the lawn and set back down on the grass. As her vision cleared Olivia could see the strong jets of water attacking the flames of the house, dousing them with the cold liquid. She blinked her eyes rapidly, the sting of the smoke hindering her ability to open them completely and she turned them upwards towards the rain to help wash the residue of the ash and smoke that lingered on her irises.

She looked up to see Nate standing over her with clenched fists and scowling down at her.

"What the hell were you thinking Miles? You broke contact! You could have died!" His eyes blazed with fury and she flinched backwards at his tone. She had never seen him this upset yet she was still too dazed and hyped up on adrenaline to fully register his anger.

Olivia wheezed, and pulled away the mask," I'm sorry Nate; I saw...I thought...I thought I saw someone."

"The house isn't clear?" He replied quickly, whipping his head up to the now engulfed structure.

Olivia coughed again and rubbed her burning eyes with her now glove-free hands.

"I don't know Nate...I looked everywhere, I swear...I think maybe they got out...saw someone running outside...then I got stuck and..."

Nate shook his head as he forced the oxygen mask back onto her face, "Breathe deep, I'll go fill the chief in."

Olivia groaned under the mask," He's pissed isn't he?"

Nate bit his lip and nodded silently.

"Shit," was all she could offer as she flopped backwards onto the wet grass.

CHAPTER 2

Olivia flinched as the chief's fist slammed onto his desk.

"Damn it Miles, you are the sorriest excuse for a firefighter that I have ever seen in my life! You broke protocol, broke radio silence and almost got your sorry ass killed in about two minutes! Not too mention you let some very expensive equipment burn to Hell while you were doing your little acrobatics out the window!"

Chief Turner had not spoken a word to her until they had reached the firehouse when he had blankly pointed for her to head into his office. Since then he had done nothing for the last ten minutes but throw insults and accusations at her, his face beet red and his eyes full of fury.

"Sir," she interrupted pleadingly, "I *saw* someone…"

"Well now that's impossible isn't it?!!" He screeched at her, "Since we just spoke to the owners and they are safely out of town! What did you see, a ghost?!!"

He clenched his fists in frustration as he glared at her mockingly, his wide forehead dripping with sweat. She would not have been surprised if small curls of smoke began to erupt from the top of his large bald head.

"If it were up to me you would have never even set one of your manicured little girly feet onto my Station floor in the first place!" he yelled.

Well, duh, she thought as she dug her fingernails into her hands behind her back, gritting her teeth tightly.

A sharp knock on the door halted his ranting and she said a silent thank you to the intruder.

"What!!!" the chief yelled, irritated by the interruption, and Olivia swore she could see daggers shoot from his beady brown eyes towards the intruder on the other side of the door.

The lieutenant poked his head in and Olivia noticed how he gave her a quick glance and then averted his eyes just as quickly. What was that look he just gave her? Pity? Probably, since she was pretty sure that all of Austin had probably heard every word that had come out of the Chief's mouth.

"We've got a situation." He replied, giving the chief a pointed look.

Chief Turner rubbed his hairy hand through his thinning black hair with an exasperated sigh. He pointed at Olivia, who stood there, slowly backing up towards the door and trying to avoid contact with him at all costs.

"You, out, go scrub the damn truck and get

out of my face!" He told her with a look that clearly stated he wasn't finished with her yet. She quickly obliged and scurried out of the office.

Olivia blew out the breath she did not even realize she had been holding as she went to hang the coat and pants up that were still stuck to her sweat soaked skin. The odor of lingering smoke was making her sick and the heat the Chief had given her in the office had brought her body temperature up more than 20 degrees, she was sure of it.

She sulked over to the truck and picked up a sponge from the bucket, wiping the smoke and dirt off of the red paint with angry, vicious swipes. Out of nowhere, a wet sponge hit her in the leg, jolting her out of her internal cursing.

"Glad to see you made it out of there alive, but you could take it a little easy on Big Red," Nate grinned as he picked up another sponge and hurled it at her.

She gave him her best glare but softened it as his expression changed to wonder. His eyes had shifted towards a spot over her left shoulder and there was a slight shadow in them she could not quite interpret.

Olivia turned to see two uniformed officers let themselves into the chief's office.

"Now what do you suppose that's all about?" Erik asked as he and Matt stalked over, both chewing away on granola bars.

Matt nudged Erik, "You know, now that I

think about it…" he chided," that girl you took home last night did look awfully young."

Erik punched him in the arm as they laughed and continued to banter back and forth as Olivia and Nate watched the officers silently.

Olivia's heart skipped a beat as the chief's door shut behind the two policemen.

She glanced over at Nate who was also looking curiously towards the closed office door. The cops rarely came around the station for an arson case. Usually the lieutenant or chief would send a report to them and they would work off of that but they usually never came in person.

She and Nate worked diligently for the next thirty minutes or so, rinsing and drying off the truck until it shined again. All the while, Olivia nervously cast glances at the chief's closed door, waiting for a sign that the meeting was finished. They were just putting the sponges and buckets away when they heard a click as Turner's door opened and the Lieutenant Sullivan poked his head out.

"Miles," the lieutenant beckoned to her, waving his hand and giving her an encouraging smile.

Olivia gave Nate a questioning look and he gave her a similar one as he shrugged. She placed the last wrung out sponge into the utility closet and headed into the office, the lieutenant closing the door behind her.

She glanced around the room and took in

the chief's annoyed face and the speculative eyes of the two officers who were currently seated at the desk. One of them was a burly but short fellow with rounded cheeks and gentle blue eyes who looked to be in his early fifties, the other a young man, probably a rookie, with blonde hair, was jotting furiously in a little notepad.

"Miss Miles, it is a pleasure to meet you, my name is Detective Gray," the older officer greeted her, standing to shake her hand with a warm smile.

As he grasped her hand he sharply glanced over at the younger officer who stopped scribbling at the silence and looked up to meet his gaze. His baby blue eyes widened and he stood quickly and shook her hand, simply offering his name as Officer Brooks and rapidly sitting back down to continue his writing.

The detective continued to stand as he offered his chair to Olivia. When she shook her head and leaned back against the wall he spoke.

"Miss Miles, we have just a few questions for you about today's incident."

Olivia glanced at the lieutenant with worry and avoided the chief's gaze at all costs although he could feel his beady eyes boring into her. Surely the police would not get involved in some kind of investigation just because she broke protocol. Lieutenant Sullivan smiled encouragingly and gestured his head towards the detective in a silent acceptance. She glanced back over at the older man and tilted her own head in question.

"You see," Detective Gray continued, "We found a body in the house that burned today."

Olivia's stomach dropped and her mouth felt as if someone had just shoved a wad of cotton down her throat.

"A body?" She whispered. Thoughts started flooding her head as her ears began to ring and she broke out into a cold sweat.

Oh my god, I missed someone. I killed someone. Someone didn't make it out of that house because of me.

"Yes ma'am," Detective Gray affirmed, shaking her out of her thoughts. "A young woman, maybe in her twenties or early teens, to be more precise was found upstairs in one of the bedrooms."

Her heart began to race as she looked at her hands which were now slick with sweat, "I thought I kept seeing someone but I looked everywhere, I swear. I walked the entire upstairs twice."

The chief folded his arms across his chest, as the younger officer nearest to her scribbled furiously in his notepad. Olivia wrung her hands nervously as her heart dropped into her stomach. Rarely was the chief the silent type and now he had all the ammo he needed to rake her through the coals, but he was just sitting there, watching her intently.

She took a deep breath to gather her

thoughts and shut her eyes for a moment, "Was the body found in the last room on the west side of the house?"

The Detective nodded and as she opened her eyes again he leaned forward intently, waiting. Olivia took a deep breath and gripped her fingers tightly as she struggled to explain.

"The closet door was open a crack," she continued, her hands beginning to shake, "I was about to inspect it but a noise down the hall distracted me and I never finished sweeping that room."

If his ears could blow smoke, the Chief looked like he was about to, but he kept his mouth shut in a tight line as the detective spoke. She had neglected to tell the chief that little tidbit, even though it would have been pointless to have attempted to get a word in edgewise earlier when he was screaming at her.

"Miss Miles," Detective Gray started, putting his hand up to calm her as her mouth opened in protest, "The young woman we found in the fire was already dead. She was found in the closet of that bedroom you described and it looked like she had been stashed there quickly. We do believe that you may have heard someone in the house, but that someone was not her, I can assure you of that."

"Miss Miles," Officer Brooks stopped scribbling and jerked her away from her thoughts, "Can you describe what you saw or heard while you were doing your sweep?"

Olivia walked through her every steps with the officers and even told them about the figure she thought she saw outside, but she was adamant that the smoke could have been skewing her vision.

"Can you describe the person you saw?" Officer Brooks asked, his eyes eagerly searching hers as he held his pen readily over the sheet of paper.

She shook her head, confused by the question, "I don't really know, I guess...I did have my mask on and the rain and smoke did make it hard to see. I didn't really see any features, I mean; I think maybe they were tall? "

The detective nodded at her encouragingly, "Anything you can remember at all will help."

Olivia cleared her throat as the light bulb finally went off in her head and her eyes widened in recognition, "You all think I saw her killer? Was he in the house when we were sweeping it?"

"We can not comment on that ma'am, that is official need to know police business," the young cop interjected fiercely.

"Brooks," Detective Gray warned, shaking his head as he shrugged apologetically, "Rookie, sorry."

The Chief mumbled something about *two peas in a pod* and Olivia had to bite her tongue as she attempted to focus on what the officers were trying to tell her.

"I'm really sorry," she replied, "but he...or she...was fast. I kept hearing noises and thought I was seeing someone but every time I tried to follow them, it was like they would just disappear. I really didn't see anything more than that. It was so smoky in there and we were in a time crunch... I...I wish I could help you more."

Detective Gray motioned to the younger police officer as he stood and shook Olivia's hand again, handing her a small white card.

"If you remember anything, anything at all," he began as she nodded her understanding.

"Do you think..." she started, and the detective stopped at the door, "Do you think he saw me?"

"That is highly unlikely miss," he reassured her, "If you couldn't even identify him as male or female, even with your gear on then there's no way he or she would even be able to recognize you. At this point we don't see any reason for you to be concerned for your safety"

Olivia glanced over at Chief Turner's glaring face and thought *'Don't be so sure.'*

He stood for a moment, his hand braced on the door frame as he looked down in thought. The detective looked back up at her as if he had suddenly made an internal decision.

"I would caution you, though, to be careful. And if you ever encounter anything or anyone suspicious I would like to be notified as promptly as possible."

She nodded and with a final farewell to the chief and the lieutenant, the officers left the office and closed the door behind them.

Olivia winced as the chief immediately bellowed out, "Back to where we left off MILES!"

"Chief," Lieutenant Sullivan stepped forward and the glaring man shut his mouth quickly. Sullivan was only a lieutenant but his years of experience always seemed to trump Chief Turner's temper. Sometimes Olivia felt like the only reason she stuck around was because Sullivan always seemed to have her back.

The lieutenant continued, "I understand, sir that Miles broke protocol by breaking radio contact and not reconnecting with her partner, however, under the circumstances I would say she did the right thing by attempting to secure the house when she felt like someone was still trapped in the structure."

The chief gritted his teeth but nodded slowly. "Alright Miles, take two days off, get some rest and come back ready to do your job right this time."

As Olivia stood there ready to argue, the lieutenant touched her shoulder lightly and as she looked at him he nodded toward the door. Reluctantly she sighed and backed down, retreating out of the office quickly before Turner could change his mind.

She stalked over to her locker in anger, grabbing her jacket and keys and muttering obscenities under her breath.

"I take it that didn't go well?" Nate innocently leaned against a nearby wall, watching her in amusement, his arms crossed over his broad chest.

With a glare she responded huffily, "I've got two days suspension, a girl is dead and I possibly may have seen her killer, so yeah, everything is just peachy."

She slammed her locker shut and stomped off as Nate jogged after her. He took her arm and wheeled her around. Her eyes locked with his in surprise as he shook her gently.

"What the hell Miles? What girl, and did you freaking say "Killer"?"

Olivia glanced at his bruising grip on her arm and flinched at his tone and he quickly released her.

"I'm sorry," he apologized as he held both hands up, "But you can't just say something like that and then walk off."

She sighed as she filled Nate in on what Detective Gray had relayed to her.

Nate whistled and scratched his light stubble, "Wow, what a twist. Do you think he, or she, saw you?"

She shook her head roughly, "No, the cops seemed pretty sure that there's no way he or she could have seen me since I couldn't even see them with my gear on."

"True, but still..." Nate replied thoughtfully,

stroking his chin.

"Freeman," Olivia said quietly, "I just want to go home and blow off some steam okay?"

He opened his mouth to reply but shut it and nodded at her, watching as she walked out of the station.

* * *

*He had cut it too close this time, and they had almost caught him. **She** had almost caught him. He needed to be quicker. Why had he decided to turn back towards the house when he had hit the trees? It was fate, he knew. He saw her there, staring out the window, an angel among smoke and flames. The danger, the rush, and the adrenaline that came with waiting to plant the body until after he had started the fire made his heart race in pleasure and excitement and now it had brought him to that female firefighter. She lived and breathed fire, he just knew it was meant to be. No matter what it took, he knew he had to have her.*

CHAPTER 3

It was late, and Olivia woke up for the third time and lay flat on her back, staring at a dark ceiling. She glanced at the clock and saw that it was only eleven o'clock at night and she groaned in frustration. She had turned in early when she arrived back at her apartment but each time she would drift off, her dreams were flooded with memories of the fire, the half-open closet door she never checked, her hands digging into the window sill as she clung on for dear life... Olivia tried to think of something else. She thought about her father, and a memory of her as a little girl popped into her head.

She had been young, about eight or so, and her father had invited her to the fire station for "Take Your Daughter to Work Day". She was sitting in his office, swiveling around in his desk chair, lifting her feet up high so that she would spin faster. Her dad had showed her around, let her honk the horn on the fire truck and she had met a few of his fellow firefighters. Now they were sitting in his office eating sandwiches for lunch and she was asking him incessant questions, as a little one typically would.

Olivia remembered asking him why he was a fireman and he had simply responded that it was his "calling". She didn't really understand what that meant at the time so she had asked him.

"It's why we are born," he answered, rubbing some mayonnaise off of his trim beard, still brown at the time, with only a few traces of gray peeking through. "It's what we are supposed to do with our lives, why we are even born on this planet."

Olivia had thought about that for a little while and her eyes had lit up.

"I know my calling!" She had shouted triumphantly, spinning around in a circle again, watching the frilly lace of her dress lift while she twirled.

He had smiled at her warmly as he asked what it was and she had responded like any other young girl would.

"I'm going to be a princess!"

Olivia's vision came back to the present and she stared blankly into the darkness. She missed those days; the carefree days when everything seemed so simple and attainable. She knew her father was proud of her but some days she wondered if the verbal abuse from Chief Turner was worth her career. With a sigh, she realized it was. She loved fighting fires, it was her passion and nothing and no one could take her from it. She wasn't a little girl anymore and from the first day she had set foot on the fire station floor as an adult, she knew that was going to be her life's calling, her forever destiny.

Her thoughts kept wandering to the dead girl, who she was, why she was killed, and more importantly, should she have done more? Tried harder to find the person, no the killer...

"No," she countered aloud as she tossed the covers away and got out of bed. She wasn't a cop and it was her job to rescue people, not to catch criminals. She slipped on some worn in jeans and finger combed her hair, pulling it back into a secured knot. She grabbed a semi-clean tank top from the floor and tugged it on, rolling her shoulders as she did to try to relieve some of the tension from the day before. Olivia needed to get out and she knew just where to go as she grabbed the keys of the counter and headed out.

* * *

Fifteen minutes later she was rolling up to the Corner Bar, parking in the crowded lot and slipping in the back door of the brick building. As she made her way through the kitchen a few of the staff waved or nodded in greeting and her stomach grumbled at the smell of fried food and grease. She had not had much of an appetite for dinner after what had happened but now that she was surrounded by delectable smells and felt as though she had not eaten in weeks.

"Hola Olivia!" Marcos called out from the grill, waving a greasy spatula at her and she headed his way. He had been with the Corner

Bar since Darcy's husband had owned it and practically ran the whole kitchen. He was thin, with olive skin, charcoal eyes and thick black hair she could never tell was styled with actual gel or just grease from all of his time in the kitchen.

"Hey Marcos," she responded as they bumped elbows in greeting and he flipped the browning hamburger patty on the grill in front of him.

"Darcy and your dad are working the bar, did you come to see them?"

"I did," she responded, "Think you can whip me up a plate of those cheese fries I can never seem to get enough of?"

He grinned and nodded, "I'll have Kate bring them out, she's handling the bar food tonight."

Olivia thanked him and left the kitchen, walked through the wood paneled space with concrete finished floors and was relieved to see that none of her fellow firefighters were hitting up the place. The last thing she wanted to do was answer a ton of questions and though they were always in jest, she knew the guys would not hesitate to at least give her a little bit of a hard time of being taken off shift for a few days.

As she headed towards the bar in the far corner, she spotted Darcy working the little register at the counter and her father right next to her, pouring some beer from the tap into a pint glass. He glanced up as she made her way over to one of the empty bar stools and smiled at her.

"Olivia!" Her father called out as she sat, "To what do we owe the pleasure hon? I thought you were on shift tonight?"

She shook her head and rolled her eyes in response as she replied, "It's a long story and I'm not sure I'm ready to hash it all out just yet. Could I get a beer?"

"Already on it," Darcy jumped in, slipping a pint in front of Olivia with a wink. One of the best things about Darcy and one of the reasons she was always so busy was her attentiveness to human emotions. She always seemed to know exactly how someone was feeling when they took a seat in her bar and today was no different. "Good to see you dear."

"You too, and thanks," Olivia responded, taking a swig of the cool liquid.

"I'll give you a minute," Andrew Miles told his daughter as he turned to take a few more orders from a young couple at the other end of the bar.

By the time she had finished half of her beer, Kate had shown up as promised, and placed a steaming pile of fries smothered in melted cheese on the bar in front of her. Olivia thanked her then immediately dug in, her appetite pleading for relief as she devoured half the plate in a matter of minutes. She watched her father work as she ate and admired his swiftness and efficiency as he took quick orders, fulfilling them promptly and hustling around the bar area.

There was no mistaking the Miles gene in Olivia as her father's appearance mirrored hers with dark, raven hair, golden brown eyes and a fire behind them that could only be matched by the ones she fought on a daily basis. Muscular and fit in his younger days, retirement had softened his build but he never seemed self-conscious of the way he looked. She sighed as he snuck a few kisses while Darcy passed or lovingly grazed her arm with his fingertips. There were times she longed for that kind of closeness with a man, but knew that with her profession it was near impossible. Chugging back the last of her beer she chewed on a fry as she stared emptily at the TV set above the bar.

A few minutes later, Andrew Miles slid into the empty stool next to Olivia and without a word Darcy replaced the beer in front of her with a fresh one. Olivia tipped her glass slowly in a toast and then chugged half of it down in a few swigs.

"Chief Turner harassing you again sweetheart?" Her father asked, turning his gaze from the robust woman behind the bar to his daughter. He chuckled as his daughter glared at her glass of beer in response.

"Suspension!" She angrily stated, gripping the beer tightly as her eyes flashed in fury, "Suspension for doing my damn job!"

Her father covered her hand with his and she swiveled her stool to face him. The soft patches of gray hair on his head and the deep lines around his kind brown eyes melted her and she struggled to keep her temper down.

"I heard about the fire today," he told her, matter-of-factly, "And for the record, I think you did the right thing." He released her hand and took a sip of his own drink as he watched Darcy serve a younger couple some sodas and a basket of nachos.

"I screwed up Dad, big time," Olivia lowered her shoulders in defeat, "I didn't complete my sweep and I put Nate and myself in danger..."

"Based on what I heard, you didn't have much of a choice."

Olivia looked at him suspiciously and narrowed her eyes as he raised his eyebrows in mock innocence as he took a drink from the glass of water in front of him.

"How did you find out about it anyway?" She accused, already having a pretty good idea of who would keep the well-known fireman in the loop about the comings and goings of his only daughter.

"A spy never reveals his sources," he responded with a goading smile.

"Oh give it up, I know it was Sullivan," she proclaimed, rolling her eyes. "It's always Sullivan."

Her dad shrugged in response.

"Come on, hon," Darcy smiled warmly as she emptied an ice bag into the freezer behind the bar. Her red and silver curls bounced as she whipped her head towards Olivia's father in an accusatory way, "Your daughter is much smarter than you're giving her credit for. Besides, we all know that you recruited Sullivan as your spy as soon as she joined the station."

Olivia lifted an eyebrow accusingly at her father as she silently dared him to try to lie to her again. If there was another thing she loved about Darcy, it was that she would side with Olivia at the drop of a hat.

"The guy thinks of you as a niece hon, he was worried."

"So nice to have all of this 'adopted family' so worried about my safety," Olivia mumbled.

"What was that?" He asked her with a confused expression.

Olivia sighed and stared at the ceiling. She thanked Darcy as she grabbed her empty fry basket and wiped the counter in front of Olivia with a wet rag.

"Oh, it's nothing. Freeman was hounding me on my way out of work today." Olivia's words dripped with sarcasm and her father shook his head.

"Now I won't have you speaking ill of one of my best recruits," her dad responded sharply, "Nate's a good man and I'm glad he's checking in on you. It takes a lot of the responsibility off my shoulders."

"Since when has everyone decided that I need to be 'checked on'? I'm a grown woman for Christ's sakes! I can take care of myself."

"Sweetheart," he coaxed, "We know you are a grown woman and that you are very independent and quite capable of taking care of yourself, but we can help but worry about the ones we love. It's in our blood. Right Darcy?"

Her father winked at his girlfriend as she wiped up some condensation from the granite countertop and she smiled warmly in response, slightly blushing. She stayed silent though, as she always did, always playing the mediator between Olivia and her dad during the few and far between arguments that they had.

"Oh please," Olivia mockingly griped, "There is just too much damn love in this place for me, I'm heading back home to pass out." She threw back the rest of her beer and left an extra-large tip on the counter for Darcy.

Her father chuckled, as did his redheaded companion behind the counter. Olivia constantly joked about how vomit-inducing their whole sappy relationship was, but they both knew that she sincerely loved the fact that her father was happy again. And Olivia was happy for him, and Darcy. But secretly, she longed for someone to be happy with and wondered if she would ever find the right guy. She kissed her dad on the cheek, said goodbye to Darcy and headed back to her apartment to pass out early.

* * *

After a sleepless night of tossing and turning she stood in her kitchen and sipped a cup of bitter coffee, looking around and shaking her head. Her place was a mess, and Olivia fully intended to use her time off to take the opportunity to clean it, as she had been meaning to do for months now.

She headed over to her closet and grabbed the overflowing bag of dirty laundry, dragging it along the floor to her washer and dryer unit in her linen closet. One glance at her semi-opened closet door took her right back to flashbacks the fire and the image of the closet she did not search crept back into her head.

"Let it go Miles..." she said through gritted teeth, and with determination she shoved clothes harshly into the washing machine. After getting those going she plugged in her old school boom box and popped in a CD of some tunes her friend Anne had given her for her birthday last year, a mixture of sixties and seventies pop hits that typically perked her spirits up. Anne and her had been friends all throughout high school and while they didn't get to see each other much (Anne was a world traveler and was currently living it up somewhere in the Caribbean), her always checked in on her when she was in town visiting her family. As she hummed and danced with the music, she worked voraciously around the apartment, picking up random items of clothing and food wrappers and vacuuming the carpet in her living room. Before she knew it, her apartment was spotless and she was dead tired due to the lack of sleep the night before and the energy she had expended working on her place. Olivia plopped down onto her recliner with a sandwich and a soda and turned on the local news, rubbing her sore feet as she sat there watching.

"Police say the body has been identified as 18-year-old Jennifer Winthrop, a recent high school graduate from Fort Worth. Her parents, James and Nancy Winthrop, had reported her missing last week, after she failed to return home from a sorority rush party. Ms. Winthrop was set to be attending Texas A&M University in the fall on a full academic scholarship."

Olivia stared at the snapshot of the beautiful woman on the screen with dark cascading curls and golden brown eyes. She had long lashes and a bright smile with pearly white teeth. Unwillingly, an image of the same woman with charred skin popped into her head and she winced as she turned from the television set.

"At this time, police say they are working on a few leads but so far they have no suspects in the case. Ms. Winthrop's body was found after firefighters responded to a house fire on Lark Lane. The homeowners were not present at the time of the fire and they do not have any connection to the victim."

Olivia clicked off the TV set and massaged her fingers deeply into her temples as she leaned further back into her chair. She tried to get the image of the girl out of her head but failed miserably. Deciding some alcohol and relaxation might do the trick, she got up and poured herself a glass of white wine and took it into the bathroom, stripping off her clothes as she went.

She pulled herself a warm bath and soaked in the lavender scented bubbles. Her hair was piled on her head and she leaned her neck back into a plush towel she had placed on the edge of the tub. The satiny bubbles kissed her skin as she felt the stress melt away into the flowery bath. She had already finished half of the wine and was just closing her eyes when a sudden sharp knock at the door had her sitting up straight, splashing water over the edge of the porcelain tub.

"Oh for the love of..." Olivia cursed as she downed the rest of her wine in a couple of frustrated gulps and slammed the glass on the edge of the bathtub with a satisfying clank. She heard more persistent knocking as she stepped out of the tub, wiping her damp feet on the rug.

"I'm coming!" She called out with gritted teeth as she quickly toweled off. She wrapped the plush towel around her dripping body, cursing again as she headed through the living room to see who had interrupted her moment of solitude. Padding over to the door, she glanced out the peephole to see Nate standing outside, holding a pizza and a six pack.

She unlocked the door and removed the latch, yanking the door open in a tiff, "Freeman, you have the worst timing!"

His startled look changed to a mischievous grin as his gaze wandered over her half naked, glistening body. "Or the best timing," he joked as she rolled her eyes and stepped back to let him in.

"Don't mind me," he continued, still grinning in amusement and placing the pizza and beer on her coffee table. "Just thought you could use some reinforcements to help you relax."

"Well what do you know?" she retorted, "That's the exact thing I was doing before you barged in here..."

"Barged? Woman, you opened the door!" he laughed as she stomped off towards the bathroom to empty the tub, grab her empty glass and change into a college sweatshirt and pajama shorts. She flitted back into the kitchen in an annoyed huff and placed the wine glass into the sink as her eyes shot daggers at Nate in the living room.

"Well just make yourself at home," Olivia snapped as she glared at the dirty shoes Nate currently had propped up on her coffee table. Her scented candle she had lit earlier once her apartment was clean was now overpowered by the stale odor of smoke from Nate's shift. She glared at him again and he just shrugged and took a swig of his beer as he handed one to her. She took it and sat down in her recliner next to the love seat that Nate had stretched across.

"You know, you are the only person under thirty that I know that owns a recliner."

Olivia leaned further back into the comfy

cushioning, "Yeah well, you just don't know what you're missing."

He harrumphed and set his beer down on the coffee table, muting the sports game he had turned on the TV as he removed his feet from her table. He folded his hands together, rested his elbows on his knees and turned his green eyed gaze towards her.

"So...how are you holding up?"

Olivia took a deep gulp of her beer. She needed to tread carefully. Nate had always been like a big brother and she knew if there was any little sign of trouble he would be camping out at her apartment, which was the last thing she needed.

"I'm good," she replied nonchalantly with a half shrug, "more pissed off than anything else. I can't believe that jerk made me take some days off. And I didn't even do anything wrong for Christ's sake! I think he would have fired me on the spot if the lieutenant hadn't stepped in to my rescue... again!"

Nate unclasped his hands and fiddled with the rubber bracelet on his wrist, "Miles, maybe you do need some time off, I mean, you almost got trapped in there, you know? When I saw you hanging there, I...well, I mean, you could have died."

Olivia ignored the shudder that threatened to flow through her and instead leaned forward and pushed her finger into his chest.

"Now look," she growled through gritted teeth, "Don't you start getting all wishy-washy on me Mister, I am perfectly fine. Did I screw up? Sure. But I had a good reason and I do not think it is fair that I be punished for that."

Nate sighed and flopped back into the couch cushions in resignation.

"I'm just worried about you Miles," he said quietly and she snorted unattractively.

Nate glanced at her and seemed to want to say something more, but he simply shrugged instead.

"You're the boss I guess."

Olivia twirled a wet strand of hair around her finger nervously as Nate stared at the basketball game on the television, a glint of anger in his eyes. She hated dismissing him but at the same time there was nothing he should be worried about. There's no way that person saw her, and even if there was a slim chance that he had, he would have known that she couldn't have made out any of his features behind a cloud of smoke and a fire helmet. The officers had already convinced her of that.

"Well hey, I've got to get going, gotta go home, sleep and then get ready for a night on the town," Nate suddenly stated as he picked up his beer and finished it in a quick gulp. He stood up and motioned towards the pizza, "You should eat something."

"Hot date?" Olivia asked, already knowing

the answer.

Nate grinned in response, a dimple forming in his right cheek. He chucked his beer into the trash can by the kitchen counter and headed for the door.

She rolled her eyes as she stood up to walk him out.

"Who is it this time? Kelly, Ashley...Barbie?"

"Ha, ha," Nate said sarcastically as stopped at her door.

As he unlocked it and stepped out into the humid evening, Olivia felt a little remorseful that she had been so defensive. She had had quite a day and a little company would not have hurt.

Stop that Miles, she scolded herself, *you're a big girl now, you can take care of yourself.*

Nate started to head towards the stairwell leading down to the parking lot and turned at the last minute, leaning so close to her that it took her breath away. In fact, she almost she swore her breathing stopped as she inhaled his scent, smoke mixed with all man.

"Lock up tight at least..." he pleaded with her, "For me?"

She sighed and leaned her head against the door frame.

"I will Nate, I always do."

Nate shook off whatever comment that he'd been about to verbalize and instead sighed and disappeared down the dark stairwell.

Olivia watched his retreating back and

then glumly closed and double locked the front door. She knew she shouldn't have been so sarcastic about his date, but Nate and the rest of the guys were casual. The job required it. No woman seemed to want to put up with the long hours those guys had. Well, no woman except for Lieutenant Sullivan's wife Jenny, and Olivia suspected that the cookies and pies she brought were her excuse to be able to see her husband more than the job allowed. Not that she or any of the guys complained about it, but Olivia knew it had to be hard putting up with hours like those.

What about me? She thought. She hadn't had a date in years, not that she ever had the time. Training and getting through the academy took up more than enough time. When she did go out for a drink, it was always with the guys and she knew that being surrounded by that many muscular males was going to put a damper on any man's attempt to get her attention.

She thought of Nate and pictured what his date must look like. Chuckling, she thought, if a man could order "the usual", it would be blonde hair, blue eyes, big boobs, legs for days. Olivia was none of those of course but she knew in general circles she was considered pretty. Being a firefighter kept her in perfect shape, and aside from a few freckles on her nose caused by a bit too much sun as a kid, her skin tanned nicely when she was able to get out of her fire suit.

Still, she had felt a slight pang of jealousy

when she thought of Nate and some bimbo together. And why had her body responded so strongly when he had been so close?

"What is wrong with me?!!" She argued out loud, grabbing her now empty beer bottle and chucking it on top of Nate's in the kitchen trash can.

Since when do I care who Nate sees? Olivia thought as she opened her fridge and poured some milk into a small plastic saucer, taking care not to spill it as she left her apartment.

He watched her as she jogged down the stairs of her apartment, the strands of hair from her ponytail flicking outwards like the flames of a well-lit fire. She reached the bottom landing and set the bowl she had been gingerly holding down on the ground near the bushes. Curious, he lifted his head a bit over the seat of the vehicle to see a mangy looking cat walk cautiously out from the bushes and begin greedily lapping up the milk.

He turned his attention to the woman, who was now hopping up the steps back to her apartment. Her toned legs flexed as she hit each step and he felt a ripple in his loins. Soon, my love, he thought, soon.

CHAPTER 4

The shrill ring of the phone startled Olivia from her sleep the next morning and she glared at the early hour the clock listed on her nightstand. She yawned and reached over to grab her cell phone, brushing her hair out of her eyes as she flipped it open.

"Hello?" she huskily answered into the phone as she cleared the sleep from her throat and sat up in the darkened room.

She listened to the quiet stillness coming from the other line.

"Hello!" She answered louder. Still the phone remained quiet. She pulled the phone from her ear and frowned at the display screen that listed *Unknown* in green letters. She growled out loud as she hit end and threw the phone back on her nightstand, settling back in to her pillows.

No more than a few seconds passed than the phone started to ring again. Her hand gripped the annoying device and she snarled in frustration.

Olivia flipped the screen open and again saw *Unknown* flashing on the screen. She answered the phone and once again was greeted with silence.

"Who is this?" She asked, attempting to sound threatening.

The person on the other end responded with a click as they hung up the call and she rolled her eyes at the sound of the dial tone.

"Nate!" She exclaimed through clenched teeth. The guys at the station were always messing with whoever had days off, trying to wake them up early or prank call them during down time at the fire house.

Olivia stretched and went to the bathroom to comb out her dark locks. They were wavy now as they had air-dried thanks to Nate's unannounced visit so she yanked through the tangles and pulled her hair up into a high ponytail. She dressed in green jogging shorts and a white tank top over her sports bra and slipped on her running shoes, grabbing her old iPod as she jogged out of her apartment to the running trail across the street.

As she stopped to stretch out her legs she inhaled the scent of the morning dew and took in the towering trees around her. She had paid a pretty penny for her apartment and it was decent but the real reason she spent so much was to have access to this wonderful running trail that had been cut out through the woods of the Austin hill country. Not only was it a pretty easy drive to work, but she loved the fact that she could live on the outskirts of a big city but be close enough if she wanted to partake in any of the nightlife or music, film and art festivals that Austin frequently held year round.

She put on her earphones and began a steady pace down the winding trail, pushing herself when she reached the uphill portions and clearing her head as she ran. She soaked in the morning sun and let the scent of wet grass fill her senses as she flew down the rocky path.

Olivia had run just about a mile when she started to feel the presence of someone behind her. She swiveled her head around and saw nothing but trail and trees behind her. Frowning she shrugged off the feeling and kept on, her tank top slick to her back with sweat.

Again she felt the hair on the back of her neck tingle and she whipped around quickly and stopped in her tracks, still seeing no one. It was pretty early still, the sun was lifting higher into the sky, and as far as she could tell no one else was out running yet. The trail curved to the right now and she could only see trees behind her from this vantage. She peered into the greenness of the forest but she still didn't see anyone.

She turned back around to continue her run and shrieked as her face smacked something solid. Strong arms held her tight and kept her from falling onto her butt.

"Jeez Miles, freak out much?"

She rubbed her sore nose and glared up

at Erik Stalle who was standing in front of her looking perplexed.

"You make it a habit of sneaking up on people?" She retorted with a glare, as she jerked the buds from her ears and let them dangle around her neck. "What are you doing out here anyway?"

"Um, I live around here, duh," he responded with a grin, "and you don't own the trail."

She took in his black running shorts and shirtless appearance.

"Sorry," she muttered, smoothing her hair, "didn't mean to bite your head off."

He held his hands up, "No worries...heard about what happened with the cops yesterday, so, a murder huh?"

"Good news travels fast."

"It does when you work with Nate. He said he was worried about you."

Olivia peered into Erik's blue eyes suspiciously, "Did he also happen to maybe ask you to go for a morning run at the exact time that I'd be running?"

"How can you even think such a thing?" Erik mockingly responded, holding his hand over his heart.

Olivia clenched her fist and squeezed her eyes shut in frustration, "Damn it, I told him to leave it alone. There's nothing to worry about!"

"Aw, I know, but you know, he thinks he's like your big brother or something and he's worried." Erik responded, as he leaned against a tree and started fiddling with his phone.

Olivia's eyes narrowed on the cell phone in his hands, "Did he also happen to mention that he would check up on me by phantom calling me in the wee hours of the morning?"

Erik looked up confused. "Um, no, he wouldn't have called you this morning. He was out late last night with the guys, we were all down at the bar until early this morning. I'm sure he crawled into bed and is probably still passed out there now."

Olivia started for a second. Didn't Nate say he had a date? She had asked him and he had smiled like he did but now that she thought about it he never had verbally confirmed it. She hated the relief that flooded through her at the thought. She shook her head of her thoughts and focused back on the attention at hand.

"Well one of you jerks woke me up early this morning," she answered roughly, wagging her finger accusingly. "And when I find out who it was, the culprit is going to get sand in his fire boots, maybe with some hidden razor blades in there."

Erik shrugged nonchalantly as he answered a text that chimed through his phone.

Probably one of the 'fire hoes', Olivia thought, smirking as she tried to jog discretely away while he was distracted.

She stopped suddenly as Erik immediately pulled up next to her and matched her stride.

"Erik," she commanded, turning towards

him and placing a hand on his chest, "Nate is not my keeper and neither are you so *please* go home before I have to hurt you."

"What? I'm just jogging here, I can't help it if it is the same way you are going."

Olivia crossed her arms and lifted her chin in defiance as Erik stood there, making a halfhearted attempt to look confused. She glared at him in silence, challenging him silently.

After a few seconds, Erik's shoulders lowered in defeat at the standoff between them and he finally nodded in acknowledgement and with a shrug and a wave jogged off towards his apartment on the other side of the trails.

With a deep breath, Olivia, no longer in a jogging mood, headed back to her apartment at a slow walk, kicking angrily at the dirt as she did and glancing back to make sure her babysitter wasn't still following her. She grumbled to herself about not being taken seriously and everyone treating her like a little girl and she vowed to get revenge on whoever interrupted her nice sleep early that morning.

As she approached her front door, Olivia took notice of a white slip of paper that had been jammed in the door frame. Assuming it was the typical house cleaning ad, or apartment newsletter, she grabbed it and tossed it on the kitchen counter as she headed to her room to change into white denim shorts and a fitted navy blue tee.

She downed a bottle of water as she dialed Nate's number and listened to the four rings and the ultimate chime of his voicemail.

"Freeman," Olivia angrily shouted into the phone, "I went out for my usual jog this morning and guess who I ran into? Oh yeah, you probably don't have to guess, since *you're* the one who sent him. I told you last night, *back off.* You're not my keeper and I'm not some helpless little girl. If you pull crap like that again we're going to have a major problem, and I mean *major!*"

She jammed her finger on the end button and slammed her phone down on the counter with a satisfying *thunk.*

Olivia held the bottle of water against her forehead, sighing as the chill of the plastic faded the heat of her anger. Her eyes drifted to the piece of paper sitting on the counter that she had plucked from the front door. She set the bottle of water down and picked up the semi-crumpled flyer and with a gasp, dropped it in horror and watched as it fluttered down onto the counter.

You forgot to check the closet.

Her heart hammered loudly in her chest as she stared in horror at the simple words typed in black on the plain white sheet of paper. She looked around her apartment quickly, as if the author of the note might be lurking somewhere in the shadows.

"It's just a coincidence," she encouraged herself, holding her hand to her chest as if that simple touch might soften the panic rising in her chest, "It could be unrelated, or a sick joke."

Olivia shook her head. Whoever did this knew about what happened at the house fire the other day. She could not imagine one of her fellow firefighters, not even Chief Turner, leaving something like this on her door. She thought back to the night before at the bar, maybe someone nearby had heard her talking to her father and thought it would be a funny prank? Unfortunately, while rare, there were some people who held caveman views about women in positions that were typically male dominated but would someone have gone to the trouble of following her all the way home from the bar to see where she lived? And then lurked somewhere out of sight until she left her apartment this morning to leave such a crude message?

Then Olivia remembered the wake up call from earlier in the morning and instantly she became more concerned. Maybe the killer had actually seen her? Was it possible that he was now stalking her? If he was, how could he have gotten her cell phone? Known where she lived?

She clenched her fists in defiance as she raised her head and took deep inward breaths in an attempt to slow her heart rate back into a normal range. She was already getting crap at work from her boss because she was a 'weak woman', she sure as hell wasn't going to take it from someone who was too much of a coward to face her head on and instead would stoop to prank calls and stupid notes.

"I am not some silly little girl," Olivia told herself aloud as the fear in her heart was overcome by anger, "I am a trained firefighter, fitter than most women and if this guy wants a fight he's going to get it."

She tossed the note in her garbage can and mentally congratulated herself on deciding not to become a victim.

The ringing of her cell phone made her jump and she shook it off as she answered.

"Hello?"

"Miles?"

Olivia sighed at the familiar voice as her heartbeat settled, "Hey Nate."

She cradled her phone with her shoulder as she screwed the lid back onto her water bottle and stuck it in the fridge, allowing Nate the chance to talk.

A few moments passed and she leaned against the counter, tapping her fingers as she patiently waited for him to speak.

Finally she heard him sigh in resignation, "You were right, I was over the line."

"Yup," she responded shortly.

"Sorry?" he offered.

She stayed silent.

"Are we still cool Liv?"

Olivia stood there and inspected her chipped, bare nails silently. He really could not help it that he had been worried. He had been looking after her for so long, it was only natural.

"We're cool," she replied resolutely with a sigh.

"Cool enough to go sailing?" Olivia could almost see the relief on his face as he spoke.

"Sailing?" she responded.

"Yeah," he replied, "Erik's got his dad's boat for the day and he's invited a few of his friends out and asked if we wanted to come."

"Sure," she replied excitedly. Maybe a day on the water would take her mind off of the note she had received plus she was very eager to get out of the apartment for a while, "What time?"

Nate told her when and where they were meeting and after they hung up she whistled cheerfully as she soaked in a long hot bath and then changed into her red bikini and covered it with her earlier outfit of shorts and a tee. If there was one thing she loved about Nate, it was that he always seemed to know exactly what she needed to cheer her up. He knew the way to forgiveness would be through sailing and after the last few days she needed a day on the water.

She flipped on the TV as she sat down to eat a quick lunch but quickly turned it off as the face of the dead girl flashed on the screen. Olivia shook her head as she pulled out the leftover pizza from her fridge and popped a few slices onto a paper plate and into the microwave.

As she sat at her kitchen table and devoured

melted cheese and pepperoni, she decided she needed to call her dad and apologize for the way she had treated him the night before. It wasn't his fault that Chief Turner was such a dick and after all, he was the only blood family she had.

"Hey there, how's my tough firefighter doing?" Her dad answered cheerfully, "You nursing a hangover?"

"Come on dad, you know me better than that," she laughed, "It would take a lot more than a couple of beers to get me trashed."

"I don't know if I should be proud or worried," he responded with a chuckle.

"Hey dad, sorry I gave you such a hard time last night," she apologized, "Chief Turner just seems to bring out the worst in me."

"He does that to everyone sweetheart, and don't even worry about it. You can't offend your old pops."

Olivia smiled.

"So what do you have planned for your final lovely day off?" He asked her and she smiled again.

"Going sailing," she said happily as she threw her empty grease stained plate into the trash.

"Aha, what did Nate do this time?" He asked knowingly.

Olivia shook her head.

"Tried to babysit me again."

"Well at least he's paying his penance."

She laughed in agreement and then told her

father she would talk to him later as she needed to still get some things together for her day on the bat.

Olivia grabbed her sunscreen, sunglasses and a hat and added it to her little bag. She slipped her feet into some flip flops and skipped out the door, the threatening note forgotten underneath the crumb filled plate at the top of her empty aluminum trash can.

CHAPTER 5

Olivia drove to the lake with her windows down, the cool breeze swiping through her ponytail and cooling her neck. As she pulled in, she saw Nate and Erik already prepping the sailboat for launch, and she envied Nate's tan skin as she took in his shirtless form. She hoped she'd get in some good rays while they were out on the water.

She hopped out of her truck and grabbed the sunscreen from her bag, slipping out of her clothes and spraying the oil-less can towards the areas not covered by her bikini. She capped the can and threw it onto her seat as headed towards the group, which included Nate, Erik, a few other guys she did not recognize and a couple of younger women who were also currently coating on the sunscreen.

As Olivia got closer, she saw that they were almost entirely ready to back the boat out. Nate turned and smiled tentatively at her approach.

"You still mad?" He asked, his knowing gaze twinkling.

"You know the way to my heart is by getting me out on the water," she replied with a smile.

"Just don't do it again," she added, with a stern look that she realized he probably couldn't see behind her dark sunglasses.

He shrugged, "I won't, I told you, and I overreacted. I worked a long shift yesterday so blame it on me not thinking clearly."

Olivia sighed and leaned against the white boat, "I wish I was working a long shift."

"Ha, no you don't," Erik cut in with a grin, "Turner was on the warpath yesterday. Besides, you're back on shift tomorrow right? Enjoy your last day off, especially with this gorgeous weather."

"You are definitely right about that," she conceded, turning her face up to the warm sunshine streaming down, "want some help backing it in?"

"We're good," Nate responded, climbing into the boat to take the reins. "Just pick a spot on the boat and Erik and I will get it going."

Olivia quickly settled into a seat on the large sailboat as Erik got in the truck to help launch the boat. Nate maneuvered the sailboat over to the end of the dock and helped Erik hop in.

"Guys, this is Olivia, she's from Station 61," Erik introduced her to the two men who were currently chatting up the women at the front of the boat. "These are my friends from college, Kyle and Graham and their wives Amy and Melinda."

"Hi," The guys nodded to Olivia and the two women slid over towards Olivia on the bench seat and shook her hand as they exchanged greetings.

Erik headed out a little bit and then put up the sails, letting the wind carry them out. The lake was smooth but the wind was perfect and Olivia inhaled the freshwater smell as she sunned herself on the soft padded seat. It was perfect, the sky was bright and she listened to the sounds of the boat rushing through the water, the soft country music playing from the stereo system and the casual conversations of Erik's friends as they all enjoyed the ride.

After a while, she opened her eyes peered over at where Nate was standing, watching as he drank a beer and helped steered the boat out of the way of a fearless jet skier. She admired his tan muscular form and took in his flat abs and his broad chest. His toffee brown hair was rumpled and her thoughts turned to what nocturnal affairs the night could have have potentially caused it. She wondered if he really had gone out with the guys or if he had in fact, actually been with some bimbo.

"So Nate," she called out to him, trying to sound casual, "how was your date?"

As she asked she took a swig of her own beer, trying her best to look like she only asked to be polite and not that she actually cared.

Nate shrugged and the corner of his mouth turned up, "Never said I had a date."

She lifted an eyebrow, "Oh? I thought last night you said you had a hot date."

He rolled his eyes in response, tossing his

empty bottle in a plastic bag and grabbing another as he sat down near to where she was lying and Erik took the boat into a cruise.

"I never said I had a date, I just let you assume," Nate said as he leaned back against the bench seat, closing his eyes and placing his muscled arm behind his head.

"Well, that's too bad," Olivia offered as she flipped down and laid on her stomach to try to even out her tan a bit. She looked up and saw Nate sitting back up and watching her intently.

"What?" she asked, bewildered, "is there something on me?" She twisted to try to see over her shoulder.

"Nope," he answered, shaking his head as if to clear his thoughts, "just wondering why you are so curious about me having gone on a date."

She tried to look disinterested, "Oh, it's nothing; just trying to make conversation, thought maybe you'd have a funny date story or something to tell to kill time but it sounds like it was just a boring night out with the guys."

Nate still did not look convinced but to his credit he dropped the subject and instead steered their conversation to the upcoming Fourth of July Parade. It was still two months away but it was the topic of conversation at the beginning of every summer.

It was tradition for Station 61 to lead the parade every year and they all loved it. It was a time to get away from the station and have kids and adults cheering for them and looking up to them. It may have seemed silly but the parade always seemed to remind them that they had a very important job and even though it only came once a year, it was a great pick me up for the team.

The chief never attended, but no one at the station was ever surprised. He said he wasn't "into those things" and that definitely was an understatement. Olivia had never even seen Chief Turner smile and the thought of him smiling and waving at a crowd of people was almost humorous. Fortunately, former Chief Miles always attended in his stead and Olivia loved being able to share the yearly event alongside her father.

After a while, Erik steered the boat into a cove, one of their favorite spots to relax, and let down the anchor. He uncapped a beer and went to hang out with his friends on the other side of the boat as Olivia and Nate continue to relax and chit chat on their end. She watched as Nate took a swig of beer, followed the hard lines of his jaw as he drank the cool liquid.

"Hey Nate?" She asked on a whim, "What's your deal?"

He glanced over at her, confused by the question.

She played with a strand of her hair nervously as she willed herself to continue.

"You know…"she coaxed, "What made you want to get into firefighting? What made you want to stay here in Austin and make our kind of salary fighting fires?"

His eyes went blank and he turned his gaze to the water as he shrugged.

"Not too much to tell," he answered and she could tell he was trying to sound casual. "When I was a kid in El Paso, before we moved down the street from your family, I used to play with this little boy almost every day. They lived right next door to us and he was my age so our parents would hang out in their driveways and we would always run around, digging for worms or whatever little boys typically do. One morning I woke up early to sirens and when my family and I went outside we saw that his house was on fire. Two story and they all slept upstairs. No one in his family made it out alive."

He sighed and shrugged, running his hand through his thick hair, "That's why we moved here. My parents were close with them and I think we all needed a fresh start. That's when I decided I wanted to fight fires. I thought I owed it to them."

Olivia solemnly touched his hand as his emerald eyes turned vacant, "I'm sorry."

Nate glanced down where her hand touched his and paused for a moment. Finally he pulled away and shrugged half-heartedly.

"It's no big deal," he continued. "If it hadn't happened I'd probably be an accountant and sitting at a desk all day or something. This life is way more exciting."

He chuckled lightly but looked away and

she took the hint and dropped the subject. Setting his beer down, he stood up and walked to the edge of the boat, gazing into the water.

"Hey!" He called out, pointing at something in the water over the side of the boat, "You gotta come see this!"

Olivia set her drink down as well and got up quickly, heading over and leaning forward to see what he was so excited about. She furrowed her brow as she peered into the clear blue water.

"Nate, I don't see any...EEEEEKK!!!" She landed with a splash into the chilly waves as Nate grabbed her and pulled her overboard with him. Olivia came up sputtering and pushing her hair out of her face as she treaded water.

"Nate you jerk!" She shouted as he laughed, backstroking casually in the water.

From the other side of the boat she heard five more splashes as Erik and his friends followed suit and jumped into the water.

"You looked hot," he answered flipping his hair up and spraying water behind him, "thought you needed a cool dip."

Olivia glared at him but stayed in the water out of stubbornness. She stuck her tongue out at him childishly and splashed some water his way as he lazed about in the soft ripples.

They spent about an hour out in the water, occasionally relaxing in silence and other times talking about work or the parade. Olivia always enjoyed spending time with Nate, he didn't over talk or under talk, he gave her space and she was comfortable with him.

As the sun started to recede and the temperature began to drop, everyone got out of the water and toweled off as Erik and Nate sailed the boat back to the dock. Once there, they hitched the boat and trailer to Erik's truck, and Olivia tugged on her tank top and shorts, admiring the nice brown tan she had gotten.

"Thanks guys, I needed this." She told Erik and Nate sincerely as she waved at Erik's friends who headed off to their own vehicles.

"What are friends for?" Nate responded with a wide grin, exposing the dimple in his left cheek. For some reason, the fact that she noticed that little feature caused Olivia to blush and she quickly looked away.

She cleared the sudden dryness in her throat and feeling the urge to leave as quickly as she could she grabbed her bag and slipped her flip flops onto her feet.

"Well," she said hoarsely, keeping her head turned to hide the flush in her cheeks, "I, uh, I need to get going. But thanks again. Thanks Erik!" she called out as he nodded to her and hopped in his truck.

She gave Nate a super quick wave goodbye and then she dashed back to her own truck and hopped in, tossing her bag onto the passenger seat and trying to put distance between them as fast as possible.

Olivia started the engine and pulled away in a hurry, leaving Nate standing alone and looking bewildered in the parking lot.

As she neared her apartment, she beat her fist down on the steering wheel. There were a million reasons not to fall for Nate Freeman. She counted them off in her head as she pulled into a parking spot and shut off the engine.

First of all, Nate was a firefighter just like Matt and Erik, and while he didn't have tons of bimbos flocking to the station like they did, she knew he dated and she couldn't imagine he would be into anything other than big boobs and blonde hair also. Secondly, he was like a brother to her, he would never see her in that way and she would be wasting her time if she tried. Lastly, Nate was after all, a coworker, and a relationship in any line of work (in her opinion) was a bad idea.

"That settles it," she concluded aloud as she opened her truck door, grabbed her bag and hopped out. A sudden squeal of tires startled her out of her thoughts and all at once the ground near her feat exploded, gravel pelting her bare legs as a loud bang echoed through the parking lot.

I'm being shot at! Olivia realized in horror as she dove back into the front seat of her truck and slammed the door, sliding quickly over to the passenger side and forcing her body deep into the floorboard. She reached onto the passenger seat for her bag and realized in horror that she must have dropped it in her haste on the ground outside.

She remained still as she tried to determine what to do next, now that her only means of calling the police was sitting in the direct path of the shooter. Olivia peeked up over the window and glanced around the now darkening parking lot, looking for any signs of a shooter or the vehicle that might be involved, but could not see much with the sun falling rapidly below the trees.

A rapid, loud banging on the driver's side window caused Olivia to shriek as she quickly cowered back into the floorboard. She shut her eyes tight and listened to her heart pounding as she waited for the inevitable bullet.

"Olivia!"

Her eyes widened and then teared up in relief as she saw Nate's concerned face staring in at her through the truck window. She hastily scrambled over to the door and unlocked it, swinging it open and throwing herself into Nate's arms, willing herself not to cry.

"What the hell is going on?" He asked frantically as she clung to him and lifted her head up to quickly scan the parking lot.

"I'm not sure but I think that someone was shooting at me!" She told him as she kept her gaze on the parked vehicles, worried that the threat might still be in the area.

Nate pulled her back at arm's length and looked her over even as she assured him that she had not been hurt. He looked quickly around the parking lot as well but there was no one around although a few people had come out of their upper story apartments to check out the commotion.

"It's okay," he comforted her as he wrapped an arm around her shaking shoulders, "Are you sure someone shot at you? I didn't see any vehicle pass me as I was driving into the lot."

She glanced around again and realized the air was deathly quiet, no cars running, no one hanging around the lot, and suddenly she felt sheepish. Closing her eyes in frustration she realized she overreacted and that she was jumping at shadows. Those teenagers in her building frequently peeled out of the lot whenever they were heading somewhere, kicking up gravel and dirt as they did. It could just have easily been the backfiring of a vehicle, but she was so jumpy she overreacted. Thoroughly embarrassed, she pulled away from Nate and reached down to grab her bag off of the pavement, shaking off tiny pebbles as she hoisted it over her shoulder.

"I'm sorry," she muttered, "I think I might have overreacted a tad." She slammed the door of her truck and turned to head towards her apartment, her cheeks flaming in embarrassment.

She let out a cry as Nate suddenly grabbed her elbow and steered her toward his truck. She wrenched her arm from his grasp and dug her feet into the pavement.

"*What* exactly do you think you are doing?" she asked him angrily, distancing herself from him. She rubbed the spot on her arm where he had grabbed her.

Nate stopped and turned in frustration, his brows furrowed in confusion.

"What do you mean what do I think I am doing? I am taking you to my place to keep you safe, and as soon as we get there we are calling Detective Gray."

"Why?" Olivia asked incredulously, "Nate, I told you, it was nothing. A car probably just backfired, it happens all the time. I am telling you, I promise I just overreacted."

"Olivia, a second ago you thought someone was shooting at you! Backfiring sounds a little different from gunshots!" He ran his fingers through his hair in disbelief at her casual tone.

"No cops Nate!" She pleaded, "Look, really, these kids that live drive like morons, they have busted up cars and they are always kicking up gravel and crap when they're leaving the lot, I'm sure that's what I heard."

Nate looked shocked, "Miles, this is your safety we are talking about here! Sure it could have been some stupid teenagers, but what if it wasn't? You can't just dismiss this as nothing."

Olivia stood her ground.

"I'm sorry Nate, but I can't just call the cops and say 'Hey I got out of my truck tonight and thought that someone was shooting at me, but it was actually a car full of teenagers peeling out of the parking lot.' They would think I was crazy!"

"Well they would be right on the money…"

he mumbled, rolling his eyes.

She glared at his words and bit her tongue, still rubbing her sore arm as she stood there in anger.

Nate's eyes softened as they focused on the slight red mark on her skin, "Did I hurt you?"

She shook her head, quickly placing her hands down at her sides, "It's fine, you just startled me, that's all. What were you doing here anyway?"

He took a step toward her and she retreated a tad.

"I am not going to hurt you Miles; I just want to keep you safe. You left in such a hurry I wanted to make sure everything was okay so I headed over here after I packed up my car. I saw your bag on the ground outside of your truck and I thought that was odd, so I knocked on your window."

She let go of her arm, "Nate, please, I know you are trying to keep me safe, but I think I am just a little edgy after the fire. Seriously, it was probably nothing. I didn't even see anything, and I am fine, really. I just got spooked over nothing, that's all."

Nate slid his hands into the pockets of his cargo shorts and after a few moments finally lowered his shoulders in defeat.

"Okay, I'll buy that you might have overreacted," he agreed, "but I think it would be best if you stayed with me for a couple of days."

She glanced over at him bewildered.

"Why?" she asked incredulously.

"Because on the rare instance that what happened was not just the result of some 'dumb teenagers'," he stated condescendingly, "you need to be somewhere safe with someone who can keep an eye on you. I don't really like you being in your apartment all alone after the cops just told you that you might have seen a killer! Besides, you just admitted that you were a little edgy."

"Nate, I can't stay with you. This is just... stupid! I'm staying here!"

"Fine," he responded smugly, "then I will just head back to my place and give Detective Gray a call."

Her mouth dropped open as he smirked and folded his arms over his broad chest.

If Olivia could have spit fire she would have but she knew Nate was stubborn, and she knew he wouldn't budge if his life depended on it. And she knew that anything he would tell Detective Gray would be a red alert on her, even if it was nothing. The last thing she wanted was someone deciding that she also probably needed to stay off the fire rotation even longer because of this whole debacle.

"I need to get some things from my apartment then." She answered roughly.

"I'll wait," Nate answered with a satisfactory smile as he leaned against his car and watched her stomp angrily off to her apartment to get a suitcase together.

Inside the apartment, Olivia threw essentials into her suitcase: clothes, toiletries, and the whole time she steamed. She adored Nate but sometimes he could be so damn stubborn and controlling. She changed quickly out of her swimsuit into jeans and a t-shirt and pulled on her sneakers.

As she stepped out of her apartment and locked the door, Nate ran up the stairs to meet her and grabbed her suitcase from her. Too frustrated to argue with his machismo behavior, Olivia followed him to his car, feeling like a prisoner being led to death's row as she walked behind him. Sure, she was probably being a little dramatic, but she just hated when people told her what to do.

She let him throw her stuff in the trunk of the sedan as she quietly got into the passenger seat, put on her seatbelt, and then crossed her arms as she turned and stared out the window into the darkness of the night, a small pout on her lips.

"Liv," Nate said softly as he slid into the driver's seat and started the engine, "I'm just doing this to protect you, you know. Not to one-up you or control you. Besides, I would feel much better if I knew you were safe at home with me."

Olivia ignored him as she averted her eyes and leaned her head on the window in silence. He sighed in frustration but kept his mouth shut as he headed the five miles to his apartment. As he drove, Olivia's eyes drifted shut to the soothing sounds of the tires on the road as they lulled her to sleep.

"Hey, we're here," Olivia felt Nate gently

shaking her awake and as she sleepily rubbed her eyes, she noticed that they had indeed arrived at his one-story country-style home. Nate had a house on the outskirts of town, a hundred acres with towering trees and the quiet that you just could not buy in the city. She had been there a few times and had told herself that one day she would have a house just like it.

She stalked out of the car, not acknowledging that he was holding the door open for her and followed him up to the house, admiring the simple white wooden structure with the wrap around porch and the soft green painted shutters. Nate had told her once that this had been his mom's house and when she had passed he just couldn't bear to sell it.

"We've got work in the morning," he informed her as they entered the home and he showed her to the guest room and set her suitcase down on the queen sized bed with the plain taupe comforter and down pillows, "So as much as I just love arguing with you, it will have to wait until we are off duty again, so for now, let's just try to get some sleep."

She gave him her best glare, hard to do, as her eyes were getting heavier with each passing second and he just chuckled and walked off shaking his head as he closed the door behind him.

Olivia unpacked her clothes into the cedar dresser and walk-in closet and took a quick shower, the sting of the gravel marks on her legs reminding her of the night's events and making her even wearier. After she toweled off she pulled on an old college t-shirt and boxer shorts and snuggled deeply under the covers, drifting off into a deep, uninterrupted sleep.

CHAPTER 6

The next morning, Olivia did her best to give Nate the silent treatment. It was hard to do, as he insisted on making them both breakfast and she *almost* felt a little guilty for being mad when he set a steaming heap of pancakes down in front of her. Almost, but not entirely, so she ate in silence and he did as well. They both got ready for work and Nate drove them, not saying a word as Olivia hopped out quickly and jogged into the station ahead of him once they had arrived.

Fortunately for her, the chief was out sick with some kind of flu, the lieutenant said. He had left the day before and had simply written a note and posted it on the lieutenant's door. Olivia perked up a bit at that, knowing that she wouldn't be yelled at, name-called or degraded during her shift.

Nate seemed to notice that she was intent on ignoring him, so he mainly kept his distance as well. She was grateful. He knew that she did not want to fight at work and she knew he didn't want to have his head bitten off in front of the other guys.

The morning was slow until a little after lunch time, the alarms started clanging and the lieutenant rounded Olivia, Erik, Nate and Dylan up to respond to a house fire a few blocks away. They suited up and headed out and Olivia couldn't shake the feeling of déjà vu as they approached a two story house that was already completely engulfed.

A woman stood in front of the house on the sidewalk, holding a baby and wailing. Her hair was disheveled and tears streamed down her cheeks as the small child in her arms screamed as well. She was wearing sweatpants and an old t-shirt and looked as if they both had just woken up from a nap.

"Ma'am," the lieutenant asked gently as he approached her, "Is this your house?"

The woman nodded as she continued to stand there and sob.

"Our new nursery, my babies clothes, our pictures, they're all gone!" She yelled mournfully as she cuddled her baby closer to her, attempting to comfort his cries as well as hers.

"Is there anyone else in the house ma'am?"

She shook her head no and sniffled as she took deep breaths to try to calm herself.

"My husband's at work. I was taking a nap with my little Ben here," she explained as she looked down at her red-faced child and tried to soothe him by rocking him gently, "when I woke up to the smell of smoke coming from the kitchen. I left my baby Ben here sleeping in his crib and headed to the kitchen which is where I saw the fire. I ran right back to the nursery, grabbed my baby and left the house."

Her eyes widened, "Oh my gosh, the stove! I had warmed his bottle earlier and I must have left it on!" The sobs racked her body as she began another bout of crying at the realization that she was the cause of the fire.

"You did the right thing ma'am," the lieutenant tried to assure her, giving a brief nod at Olivia as the men began to work on dousing the flames.

Olivia obeyed the silent order and wrapped a gentle arm around the woman, urging her further away from the fire to an approaching ambulance and ignored the lady's protests between sobs and hiccups that she and her baby were perfectly fine. The ambulance pulled to a stop and Olivia handed the woman and her baby over to the paramedic and they immediately wrapped a blanket around the both of them to calm the two.

She headed back to the house and helped her fellow firefighters spray down the fire. The smoke turned black and billowed into the air as the flames were slowly extinguished and all that remained was a charred shell of what used to be the woman's house. After a while, once the fire was completely put out, and their equipment put away, the exhausted firefighters piled into the truck and headed back to the station.

As she was putting her gear back up, Olivia

heard a familiar voice. She turned and spotted Detective Gray heading with the lieutenant into his office and shutting the door.

"This is getting to be a theme with you, huh Miles?" Erik teased her as she rolled her eyes at him and gazed at the closed lieutenant's door nervously.

They all worked on cleaning the truck, but Olivia could not help throwing glances at the lieutenant's office, wondering why the Detective was back and what information he might have.

Finally, the door opened and Olivia set her sponge down, expecting to be called in, but as she watched, the detective thanked the lieutenant and then left the station, giving her a brief nod as he did. Olivia walked straight over to the lieutenant, intercepting him as he attempted to head back into his office.

"What did Detective Gray want?" Olivia asked him curiously, touching his arm lightly.

He looked anxiously around as some of the guys perked their heads up to hear, "Nothing really, just a follow up on the other day that's all." He shrugged and turned to walk into his office but she grabbed his arm.

"Lieutenant, please," she pleaded.

He looked torn and then nodded resolutely as he motioned for her to follow him into the office. She obeyed and when she entered he shut the door and gestured for her to have a seat as he took his own behind his desk.

"They found another body," he told her simply, watching her intently for her reaction. Olivia's breath caught and she gasped aloud.

"Where?" She asked, "Not the house we just…"

He shook his head rapidly, "No, not there. They found this one in a fire on the outskirts of town. An old mobile home that had been abandoned. Station 63 handled that one."

"Are they thinking it's the same person that killed the young woman in the fire we put out?"

"They are not positive yet until they get an ID on this new body but they wanted to alert us right away just in case we can remember anything else that might help. The cops are not too happy that the media got wind of that other girl turning up dead the other day and they are nervous that this will leak before they can ID the victim, so mum's the word or my job is on the line."

"I won't say a word," Olivia assured him, but inside she was frightened. Two bodies? Olivia wasn't sure, but this was sounding more and more like a serial killer. And she definitely did not like the fact that it involved two fire stations in the Austin area.

"Alright, now get out there before anyone thinks anything is wrong," the lieutenant ordered her and she nodded and scurried out. Fortunately for her, the guys were busy finishing up the truck and her absence went pretty much unnoticed.

The rest of the morning went on without a

hitch, save for Erik and Nate having to run out to respond to a small grass fire and a vehicle fire that had caused a mess of traffic near the university but other than that, it was a relatively quiet day. Olivia spent a lot of time working out, trying to relieve the tension and stress of the past week by burning calories and lifting weights.

At about three that afternoon a small class of elementary students came traipsing up the driveway, their little faces shining with joy at being able to actually see real firefighters and fire trucks. The lieutenant came out of his office and greeted Mrs. White, the school's fourth grade reading teacher and also her father's neighbor.

"Hey kids," Erik waved as he came out in full garb, save for his helmet. This was typical with school visits to the fire station. It was important that small kids get to see that firefighters are really just people under all of that gear, so that they could trust them in the event they were in a real fire emergency.

"Oh, my dear Olivia!" Elizabeth White exclaimed as the kids oohed and aahed over the helmet Erik passed around. She wrapped Olivia up in a huge hug and kissed the air next to her cheek.

Olivia had always liked Mrs. White, she was a very nice woman with a passion for teaching and she was frequently dropping off roses from her garden to Darcy at the bar when she had a good bloom in. However, her and her husband also had the biggest ears in the county and they loved getting and spreading gossip wherever they could. Olivia could not help but think that it was such a huge coincidence that her class was visiting Station 61 after what had been on the news.

"How are you Mrs. White? I haven't seen you in a while?" Olivia returned the hug and then had to side-step a little girl who had run past her to check out the fire truck.

"I'm perfectly wonderful sweetheart, as usual."

The older, lean woman grasped Olivia's hands firmly in hers and leaned forward suddenly.

"I heard about what happened you poor thing," she quietly muttered, glancing around to make sure her voice was low, "Please let me know if there is anything I can do for you."

"Thank you Mrs. White," she sighed, "But I assure you, it was no big deal and I am perfectly fine."

"I can not believe we have a murderer in our midst," Mrs. White exclaimed, as she fanned her face dramatically, "I told Harold that we need to install a deadbolt on our front door immediately. And to get out his old shotgun too of course. Do the police know who did this?"

"No ma'am," Olivia answered, "I am sure they are working hard to find out who did it though, so I'm sure you will be fine."

"Do you know how the woman died?" Mrs. White asked, leaning towards Olivia expectantly, eyes gleaming, "the news didn't say but Miss

Annabelle at the school says that she heard that it was a sledgehammer that did it."

"I really don't know any of the details Mrs. White," Olivia answered patiently, trying to look as in the dark as she really was.

Mrs. White stood there a minute searching Olivia's face suspiciously, but then she finally shrugged.

"Well I am still going to get some extra security going at my house, you just cannot be too careful nowadays."

"I'm sure you will be just fine," Olivia assured her as she tried to subtly head closer to the truck and the kids gathered around it. She looked up and saw Nate smirking at her knowingly as kids tugged at his t-shirt and she glared at him in response.

Fortunately at that moment a little boy ran up to Mrs. White and asked to use the bathroom and Olivia was free to head towards the school group and away from the interrogation.

After the kids had left, a few hours had gone by and finally their shift ended and Olivia and Nate headed home together in his car in silence. Olivia leaned her head back in exhaustion. She knew her work day had been semi-slow, but the fire earlier and the subsequent information about the newest dead body took a toll on her emotions.

As Nate pulled into the long dirt drive, he shut off the ignition and turned to her.

"Are you talking to me yet?" He prodded,

with an amusing tone.

She looked back at him, un-amused.

"Nate, I am exhausted, can we just come back to this tonight, once we have both gotten a good nap in?"

He nodded in agreement but seemed satisfied that she had actually answered him so he whistled as they went into the house and to their separate rooms to crash.

Olivia scrubbed the smoky smell from her body and hair and as she always did directly after a shift, and got her second wind so she took the time to blow dry her hair. She changed into a tank top and boy shorts and settled onto the bed to watch some daytime TV until she drifted off to sleep.

He watched the girl in silence as she stared up at him with wide eyes, tears running down her face, her mouth silenced by a white cloth. She sat there on the hard concrete and he could see her struggling against the rope that secured her wrists behind her back. He paced in front of her like an animal stalking his prey and she sank back against the wall as if she could disappear into it.

This one was even prettier than the first two, with full pouty lips and bedroom eyes. Her dark silky hair was almost black and hung almost to her waist. The best part however, was her voluptuous figure; Too slim for an adult but too curvy for an adolescent teen. Her breasts strained forward, almost protruding out of her low cut top and her skirt ended right below the curve of her hips. Oh yeah, she was definitely asking for it. He would have taken her but he was already spoken for by his angel of fire. This one was just for fun.

He had watched them all as they partied, drank, danced and groped. Teenagers, celebrating their freedom and lowering their inhibitions. He watched as she brushed off advances from several suitors but he knew better; she was playing hard to get. They all played hard to get. But she wanted it, he knew that she did. He could tell by the way she dressed, the way she had danced suggestively with her female friends. So he had waited in the dark. She had been abandoned by her friends who were either passed out or went home with the teenage boys that had fed them the alcohol.

He had watched her stamp her foot like a stubborn child when her last ride left and he followed her as she had decided to walk home alone. It really was easy; she made it easy. They all did.

She whimpered as he approached her holding the knife. He ran the blade slowly down her neck and smiled triumphantly when he nicked the delicate skin and she cried out in pain. Her hands shot out in front of his face and he growled as sharp nails raked across his cheek. Angrily, he punched her in the face repeatedly until the blows knocked her out. Satisfied, he grabbed the gas can and started drenching her body and the room with the strong liquid. Then he lit a match.

CHAPTER 7

Olivia struggled through the thick smoke as she saw the dark shadow dart from the little girl's room. She ran the opposite direction, intending to get away from him this time. As she did her mask started to fill with smoke. "Freeman," she called out frantically, "I have a leak!"

She looked around quickly and saw one single door, the door to the little girl's room, but it was closed. Olivia grabbed the handle and pushed, but the door would not budge and her mask was filling with smoke.

She turned around and her only other exit was now blocked with angry red and yellow flames.

"Nate, I can't get out!" She choked out in a strangled voice.

She rammed her body into the door as hard as she could but it wouldn't budge. The smoke in her mask filled her lungs and her eyes teared up in agony. Olivia slammed into the door one more time and this time, it flung open and she stumbled into the room.

She regained her balance and as she looked up she was face to face with a large man dressed all in black. A silver revolver was pointed directly at her *face.*

"Game Over." He said as he pulled the trigger and Olivia screamed.

She awoke to someone holding her arms down and she continued to scream, struggling against her attacker.

"Miles, it's me, calm down!" Nate's frantic voice jolted her back to reality and she quickly lowered her hands, grimacing at the tiny scratch marks she had made on Nate's tan arms.

"I'm sorry," she said softly as she quickly sat up and tried to push back the fear that her dream had caused.

"I've had worse," he shrugged with a half-smile, and she saw that he was wearing a t-shirt and boxers. Realizing her own half-clothed state she quickly tugged the covers up to her chest and made a feeble attempt at smoothing her bed-head hair.

"I woke you up?" she asked, more of a statement than a question.

Nate sat next to her on the bed and shrugged again. His hair was disheveled, sticking up all over the place, and Olivia imagined him on top of her working himself into a sweat.

Where did that thought come from? She shook her head to clear it and hoped it was dark enough for the flush on her cheeks to not show.

"Yeah, but I needed to get up anyway."

She really needed to push those thoughts out of her head, especially around Nate.

He inspected her face curiously as she squirmed under his scrutinizing stare.

"Are you okay?" Nate asked her with concern and she nodded.

"Just a stupid dream, no biggie." She said, trying to appear unaffected. "Sorry for the drama." She inspected a loose thread on the comforter and silently avoided his gaze.

"Are you sure?" He probed, softly grasping her chin in his fingers and tilting her head up to meet his.

"Drop it Nate, please." She pleaded, wrenching back from his grasp.

He growled in resigned defeat as he got up and headed back to his room muttering something about stubborn woman. Olivia buried her face into the pillow, hiding her beet red cheeks.

She was so embarrassed at the fact that she actually screamed out loud in her sleep and for thinking such sinful things about him when she was supposed to be mad at him; and when she had resolved not to think of him that way. She definitely needed something to distract her from thinking about the fire *and* Nate Freeman.

Olivia got out of bed and checked her phone and perked up at the text on the screen. Her friend Anne was finally back home from her Caribbean vacation and was dying to meet up.

"That is just what I've been needing," she said aloud, "Some good girl time and some good drinking!"

She dialed her friend's number and Anne squealed in delight when she answered. Olivia sighed with contentment as she welcomed the overly cheerful nature of her friend's voice on the phone.

"How was your trip?" Olivia asked. This simple question opened the floodgates and for the next twenty minutes Anne dished about the Caribbean hotties, the clear blue water and the fruity drinks she had spent all week sipping. Her career as a travel agent made it so that she was able to spend a lot of her time visiting resorts on their dime and she took full advantage of it. She was a free spirit and Olivia knew that no other job would have been more perfect for her best friend.

"Girl, I am so sorry, I am just going on and on as usual," Anne apologized, "I'm so selfish. How was your week?"

Olivia simply sighed.

"Uh oh," her friend answered knowingly. "You want to head to Corner Bar in thirty minutes? Pick me up?"

Olivia agreed quickly and she hung up with her friend so that they both could get ready. She was glad she had grabbed some of her "going out" clothes when she had packed for her prison time with Nate and quickly dressed in a denim frayed mini-skirt, black halter top and black strappy sandals. She ran a brush through her hair and went with a smoky eye on her lids and simple gloss on her lips.

Satisfied at her appearance, Olivia opened the door to the hallway and pressed her ear against Nate's bedroom door. The sound of a shower appeased her and she quickly hurried out the front door, grabbing his car keys as she went. She drove the fifteen minutes to Anne's house and honked as she approached the small split level brick home.

Olivia's face lit up as Anne ran down the front steps and hopped in the truck.

"Oh my goodness, your tan looks gorgeous!" Olivia gushed at Anne's now bronzed skin. Anne was pretty, not necessarily beautiful, but girl next door attractive with freckles, strawberry blond hair and green eyes. Her hair was short and cropped and she had what you would call a "curvy" figure.

Anne buckled in and Olivia watched her curiously as her friend's gaze went from confusion, to surprise and ultimately to glee.

"What?" She asked, bewildered.

"I was wondering whose car this was! You and Nate finally took the plunge didn't you??? Oh, I'm so happy!!!"

She threw her arms around Olivia, causing her to jerk the wheel a bit. She recovered and then glanced at her friend in astonishment.

"Um, Anne, what are you babbling about?"

She leaned back, confused. "Well, you're driving Nate's truck so I figured you and him…"

Olivia put her hand up quickly, "First of all, a lot of stuff went down while you were on your trip. And secondly, Nate and I aren't together."

She filled her in on the events of the week, omitting the part about the note, and the silent phone calls, still trying to convince herself that those were just harmless pranks.

"But Nate's cool with you going out then?" Anne asked, skeptically.

Olivia bit her lip and stayed quiet.

"Liv! He's going to be so pissed!" Her friend laughed with glee. "Dang! I was so hoping that when you picked me up in this you were going to tell me you were like, sleeping with him or something."

"Anne, why would you think or be hoping for that?"

"Oh come on," she said, with a skeptical tone," you mean to tell me you don't see that way he looks at you on the rare occasion we drag him out to a bar, or the way he always wants to protect you, like now, basically forcing you into living with him."

Olivia brushed off her comments but her stomach flip-flopped as she focused on picking a good spot near decent lighting in the already crowded parking lot.

"He sees me like a sister Anne; he doesn't like me that way. I think he just enjoys being a control-freak older brother type since he never had any siblings. Besides, who says I'm interested in him?"

"Okay," she dragged out the word slowly

and sarcastically, with a hint of amusement in her eyes.

"What?!" Olivia asked her as Anne's lips curled up into a smile.

"Nothing sweetie," she responded, "let's just enjoy our night out...you've earned it. I cannot believe that jackass of a chief made you take some days off after you did *your job!*"

"I know, he's so damn frustrating!" Olivia agreed in earnest, "I mean, he has been looking for any reason to get rid of me and if the lieutenant hadn't backed me up I think he was going to try to fire me that day!"

Anne shook her head, "What an asshat."

"But Liv," she continued, looking at her friend with concern, "How are you? I mean, a girl was killed and stuffed in that house like trash. And you might have seen the guy and maybe he saw you! I can't even imagine. I would be soooo paranoid!"

"Well Nate definitely is," Olivia muttered, then she answered Anne, "I just think the whole thing is a fluke. I didn't see any of his features and I'm sure they could not have seen me clearly, so it's not my problem anymore you know? If I wanted to be a cop I would have gone to school for that instead of becoming a firefighter."

Anne nodded in agreement and touched up her lipstick in the rearview mirror. She smacked her red lips together then turned and grinned at Olivia.

"Well, let's have a great night and help put it all behind you!"

The bar was already pretty crowded and it was only ten o'clock. They walked in and Dylan Rider and Erik called them over to some empty stools by the bar. As they headed over, Olivia looked around but she didn't see any signs of her father or Darcy. She knew that meant they were taking a night off for themselves and she breathed a sigh of relief. She loved Darcy and her father but tonight she needed a bit of carefree dancing and drinking, and having her dad and his girlfriend around to watch her would have been way too awkward.

"Nice tan, Caribbean Mama, looking good!" Erik whistled at Anne and she blushed furiously as she quickly ordered a few tequila shots with lime.

"Starting early huh?" Dylan asked Olivia as she took a seat. "Heard the chief was pretty tough on you the other day."

"It's alright," She shrugged it off, "My battle wounds are almost healed. You should see his."

Dylan laughed, "Yeah, you must have done a number on him, making him sick and all that. I don't think he's ever taken a day off in his life, let alone multiple days!"

"Chief Turner skipped work because he's sick?" Anne replied with disbelief. She knew all about the fire station chief's habits firsthand from Olivia's venting.

"I know!" Olivia agreed, "I was surprised too,

but it made for a great workday yesterday. I didn't have to worry about getting fired all day. The lieutenant said he had the flu or something."

"I bet he's got ass-hole-i-tis." Erik responded smartly.

"Then he must have caught it from you!" Dylan said, punching him on the arm with a chuckle as he tossed back the rest of his glass of beer he was holding.

"I bet "Runt" Miles over here feels really sorry for the guy!" Erik said with a laugh as he punched Dylan back.

Olivia rolled her eyes as she downed the tequila shot that had been placed in front of her, sucking on a lime wedge after and licking the corner of her mouth to remove the remnants of salt that lingered there. Anne followed suit and ordered two more as the music in the bar got louder and more people started filling up the bar.

"Mrs. White came by with her fourth graders too," Olivia told Anne with an eye roll.

"Oh great," Anne replied knowingly, "Did she ask about the murder, the chief, your personal life? Was the little nosy body hunting for information as usual?"

"She was trying to get information but to her credit she backed off pretty quick when I kept being short with her. She is all up in arms about 'getting her house to be safe' because she 'doesn't want to be next.'"

"That woman is nice but damn does she

love being the center of attention," Anne stated with a sigh.

Four shots and many beers later, Erik was, as usual, flirting with some blond chick in the corner and Dylan, Olivia and Anne were trying to come up with other creative illnesses that could have befallen Chief Turner. A sexy hip hop song started and a tall, raven-haired guy asked Anne to dance, leaving Olivia and Dylan alone with their drinks.

"Get out here guys!" Anne yelled at them as Erik and his blond also made their way out to the bumping and grinding intertwining of bodies on the dance floor.

"Well?" Dylan asked Olivia as she sipped on a too-sweet cranberry vodka concoction.

"Oh, I don't know," she responded, biting her lip nervously as she watched the tangle of bodies on the dance floor.

Dylan held his hands up, "I won't bite, I promise."

She took a deep breath and followed him out on the dance floor, careful not to accidentally touch any of the gyrating hips and bodies that engulfed her as she moved deeper into the crowd.

As the strobe lights and music flowed through her, Olivia started to move to the upbeat music, closing her eyes and letting her stress go as everyone laughed and danced around her. Finally her worries and the anxiety from the recent events faded to the back of her mind as she floated with the buzz from the alcohol. She chuckled as Dylan slapped Erik on the butt and moved with the music, trying to keep a safe distance from everyone around her.

"Oh shit," Dylan cursed looking over her shoulder and Olivia turned around to see Nate standing behind her, glaring at Dylan with his hands fisted firmly on his hips.

"Um, we were just dancing man," Dylan told Nate, holding his hands up in surrender, "Just having a little fun, that's all."

Olivia stopped dancing and looked at Dylan, confused, "What are you talking about? He's just pissed off because I took his car."

"Is that right?" Nate asked hotly as he took her arm roughly and guided her off the dance floor, leaving Dylan behind looking sheepish. Olivia's feet tripped on the wood slick with spilled drinks as she struggled to keep pace with him.

"You took his car?" Erik laughed in disbelief behind them. Nate clenched his jaw and ignored him as he shoved his way through the sweaty grinding bodies to an empty area in the corner of the bar, tugging Olivia with him.

"What the hell do you think you are doing?!" He shouted incredulously over the music and she flinched at the volume of his voice, "You stole my car, picked up your friend and came to a bar where anyone who wanted to kill or kidnap you could do it!"

"I am not here by myself Nate!" She

retorted, rolling her eyes and sticking her lower lip out in a pout. She knew she looked childish but the combination of liquor and the stress of the last week had her frustrated with his tone.

"And you think that makes you safe?!!" He asked in disbelief, staring back at her as though she just landed on Earth from another planet.

"Yeah!" she shouted back angrily.

They came to a stop and he spun her around quickly and pulled her hard against him.

"Look around you," he continued, breathing into her ear as her body warmed with his closeness. Her heart pounded, and she became flushed as she felt him curve into her.

He pointed at the bar, "There, see, are the drinks that young bartender just brought for you and Anne. Out in the open, unattended and you were probably just going to down it when you finished dancing, no matter what drug might have gotten slipped into it while you weren't looking."

Nate swiveled her to look towards the dance floor and the crowd of people who were dancing hypnotically with the loud music.

"And there you have Anne, who came with you, but who will probably end up leaving with that guy who's trying to shove his tongue down her throat. Strike two, Miles."

"What's strike three then? Erik and Dylan are here, aren't they?" She challenged, not so strongly anymore, her voice heavy with alcohol and her words slurring slightly.

"Erik takes home miss blond one-night-stand there, leaving Dylan, who is way to drunk to be trusted with you right now. I saw the news tonight Miles, I know that they found another dead woman at a fire earlier today and I don't understand why you are being so careless about this."

Olivia wrenched clumsily from his grip and then wheeled around to glare at Nate as she pointed her finger at him, attempting to stay steady on her feet even though the quick turn had made her dizzy.

"Now look here damn it, I am so done with this big brother crap! It is none of your business where I go or what I do. You are not my keeper so stop acting like it!"

"It is my business, as your friend, that you are safe. And you are putting yourself in a position where you're not! This guy has killed two women already and you may have seen him. You are not safe here!" He angrily retorted, his green eyes flashing to a dark jade color.

"I'm not alone! Like you said I can leave with Dylan. And what is it to you if we end up so drunk that we do something stupid like, sleep together? I *am* an adult, Nate; I can sleep with whoever I want to."

Nate's face fell and his shoulders drooped as he went silent.

"So you're into Dylan all of a sudden huh?" He asked quietly as he ran his hand through his hair, looking at the ground, his mouth twisted into a bitter scowl.

"Maybe," she said, pouting with her arms crossed, "And who said it was all of a sudden?"

Nate whipped his head up to glare at her, his eyes flashing with fury.

"Fine, have your fun, but give me my damn keys or I'll call it into the cops that my car was stolen, and then they can keep you safe in a jail cell."

Olivia's hands shook as she reached into her skirt pocket and dropped the keys into Nate's hands. She couldn't tell if the knot in her throat was from all the mixed liquor she had had or from something else entirely. Nate turned without a word and stomped out of the bar, leaving her speechless and shaken.

"Hey," Dylan said, coming up beside her. "Everything okay?"

"Yeah," she responded, "He's just not too happy that I took his car without asking."

"He'll get over it," Dylan shrugged, grabbing her hand and leading her back to her friends, "Let's get back out there!"

Olivia obliged, following Dylan back into the crowd, but she couldn't help but throw one last look towards the door Nate had stormed out of.

CHAPTER 8

Olivia woke up in the morning with a pounding headache and a guilty conscience.
She knew she shouldn't have been so mean to Nate. He really was doing her a favor by taking her in when he didn't have to. And here she was acting like a surly, rebellious teenager. That would have definitely explained his enraged reaction last night, and as much as she hated to admit it, he was entitled to it.

After a quick shower, she dressed in jeans and a t-shirt and headed to the kitchen, fully prepared to make a greater effort to be nicer *and* to apologize for the night before, but Nate wasn't anywhere to be found. She walked back to his bedroom, where his door was wide open, the bed unmade, sheets rumpled on the floor. His window was slightly open and a slight breeze ruffled the blanket that was haphazardly strewn on the mattress.

Olivia sighed and stalked back to the empty kitchen. She busied herself by making a cup of coffee, sipping the hot caffeinated beverage as she left the house to sit on the wooden bench by the front door. As she tucked her legs underneath her she noticed that Nate's car was gone.

He probably had some errands to run, she thought to herself, slightly worried that he was just keeping himself busy in an attempt to avoid her.

She had been pretty messed up last night. She took his car, making him pay for a cab ride to a bar in the middle of the night to find her, and as much as she hated to admit it, had put herself in a position of danger in the event someone was indeed looking to hurt her. AND she basically made him believe she was a slut, the way she talked about sleeping with Dylan.

Her night out had been ruined and she sighed as she realized that while she wanted to blame Nate, it was entirely her own fault. She had spent the rest of the night half-heartedly drinking and dancing only to make Dylan leave their friends early to drop her off because she just wasn't having fun anymore. And poor Anne, on her first day back from vacation was stranded with the guys, not that she minded, as drunk as she was. Fortunately Dylan had headed back to the bar and had promised to make sure her friend would make it home alright as well.

She stroked a finger along the deep lettering of the mug she held and sighed. Would she have gone home with Dylan if Nate hadn't come along and played big brother? She certainly had been drunk enough, Dylan wasn't unattractive by any means, and good Lord it had certainly been so long since she had had sex that it was an itch that definitely needed scratching. They would have had a quick tumble and by the time work came around it would have been as though nothing had happened. That was how most of the guys at the station spent their nights. No attachments, no upset girlfriends or wives when they were gone for 24 hours or more at a time.

Olivia leaned back on the bench as she thought about Anne's reaction the night before when she had showed up in Nate's car. Accepting defeat against her inner thoughts, she sighed. Of course she had a thing for Nate. She always had. But he had always portrayed the "big brother" vibe, never the "girlfriend" vibe. There was no way he was into her and she was not about to make things awkward by going after someone who was inevitably going to turn her down. And the embarrassment of seeing him at work after something like that would be massive.

Olivia finished her hot brew and headed back inside, washing the mug and putting it back in the cabinet. She glanced outside the window again and saw that Nate's sedan was still missing so she shrugged and settled onto the couch with a magazine. As she flipped through the beauty ads, her phone chimed.

'You alright hon? Saw you left early, everything okay?'

Olivia typed up a quick text back to Anne telling her that she had just gotten tired the night before but that she was fine. A lie of course, and she knew Anne probably knew it, but one of the best things about her friend was that she knew when to leave well enough alone.

Her phone rang and she her head throbbed from the shrill sound.

"Morning dad," she answered with a yawn as her father's voice greeted her cheerily on the other line.

"Hey sweetie, are you okay? Darcy and I went by your apartment this morning to drop off some peach pie that she made but no one answered."

Crap! Olivia smacked her hand to her forehead as she realized she had not even thought to call and tell her father where she was.

"Dad, I am so sorry, I should have called you," she apologized, "I've been staying at Nate's house."

"Oh, um, well, that's, um, that's fine sweetie," her father stammered in response. Olivia's cheeks reddened as she realized that her words had come across wrong and why her father was suddenly so uncomfortable.

"No dad," she responded, "It's nothing like that, I'm just sleeping in the guest room. Anne came home yesterday and uh, we had a late night out with the guys at the bar and Nate lives closer so..."

She realized she was rambling. She didn't want to worry her father by telling him the real reason she was staying at Nate's and hoped her excuse would appease him.

"Oh," her father replied, sounding a tad relieved, "I understand. Well, we brought the pie back home so whenever you get a chance, stop by and visit and you can pick it up then."

"Ok dad," Olivia agreed, "Love you."

"Love you too sweetheart," he responded as he hung up the phone with a click.

Olivia blew out a deep breath. She hated lying to her father but she did not see the point of worrying him with simple speculation.

The sound of tires on gravel made Olivia's heart jump, but when she spotted the familiar car outside her breathing settled. It was not until she heard the door knob turn that she remembered Nate's demeanor the last time she had spoken to him. She looked quickly around and realized she would look like an idiot if she took a running leap towards her room so she settled for burying her nose back into her magazine.

Olivia did her best to ignore Nate as she heard him bring some bags into the kitchen and start opening and closing cabinets, putting the groceries away. As she heard the rustle of plastic, she risked a peek at him, albeit a quick one, and fortunately he was facing away from her at that very moment. She took the opportunity to admire his physique in a plain white t-shirt and snug jeans and quickly turned back to her magazine when he began to turn towards her.

She scolded herself for being such a coward, and finally, she looked up at him and took a deep breath.

"Hey Nate? I'm, um, I'm really sorry about last night. I should not have taken your car and I should have told you where I was going so that you wouldn't have worried."

He took his eyes off of the can he was currently holding and looked up at her silently, almost smugly, but she noticed there was questioning in his gaze.

She sighed in defeat and slumped down in the soft cushions, looking down at her hands absently as he stood there in a long drawn out silence.

"At least you got home alive...Dylan drive you?" He asked finally, startling her with his acknowledgement.

"Yes," she answered and as she looked back at him, his jaw was set in a firm line and he averted his gaze and began studying the ingredients on the can he was holding as if they held the secret to life itself.

"I didn't sleep with him if that's what you're thinking."

"Miles, I could care less who you sleep with," he answered roughly, tightening his grip on the can and slamming it into the open cupboard.

Olivia could feel her heart crumbling deep in her chest. She knew that he had always seen her as a sister but somehow hearing verbal proof seemed to cut her deep. It was obvious that he was not interested in her in that way and now their friendship was even at stake.

As he put the last of the groceries away, Nate grabbed his keys and headed to the door. He kept his back to her as he spoke.

"I've got to get the car gassed up," he told her gruffly, "Be back in a bit."

Olivia shuddered as he slammed the door behind him, the sound echoing around her as though he had just shoved his fist into her heart.

"Great going Olivia Miles," she told herself aloud, "Not only do you not have a shot at Nate romantically, but if you are really lucky, he will never forgive you and your friendship will go down the toilet too."

She slapped the magazine down on the couch and decided to head back to her room to charge her phone while she watched some TV to relax.

As she headed down the hallway she stopped just outside her room and frowned in confusion.

I don't remember closing my door, she thought as she placed her hand on the doorknob.

Just as she began to twist, she heard the sound of breaking glass from the other side of the door and a jolt went through her.

Olivia quickly turned and tore off towards the kitchen, grabbing the butcher knife from the silverware drawer as she passed. She desperately looked down at the phone in her hand and to her dismay the screen was now black.

She backed slowly up towards the front door, all the while keeping an eye on the closed door to her bedroom and listening to any evidence of an intruder on the other side. As her foot landed on an unstable board with a slight creak she winced and froze in place, afraid that she had been caught.

She took a deep shuddering breath and another step back, but this time she bumped into something solid and yelped. A hand grabbed the wrist of her hand that held the knife and another hand covered her mouth. She made a fist with her free hand and prepared to swing back towards the culprit's groin.

"Shh, it's just me," she heard Nate whisper.

She relaxed as he let her go and motioned for her to stay back as he pushed her safely behind him and crept towards the closed door, turning the knob and quickly wrenching the door open. He disappeared inside the room and Olivia's heart pounded with fear as she hugged the wall and stared at the open doorway, too panicked to move.

A few moments went by and Olivia didn't hear anything so she slowly moved toward the open bedroom door. She peeked in and saw Nate crouched over some glass that had fallen from the now broken window.

"Nate?" She called out tentatively.

He stood and faced her, gingerly holding a

shard of glass.

"Whoever it was, they're long gone by now. I saw some footprints leading out to the woods. Fortunately for us though they left some DNA when they broke the window, get a bag from the kitchen will you?"

She obliged and when she brought the sandwich bag back he placed the piece of bloody glass in it and sealed it. Olivia took a moment to look around and saw that some of her clothes had been strewn all over the room and ripped to pieces. Her makeup box was on the floor and a tube of red lipstick lay next to it.

It was then that she saw the red letters on the white bedroom wall.

'Soon, my Angel of Fire'

Olivia's stomach churned and she placed a hand over her mouth to keep her coffee down. She stood there, frozen in place, as she attempted to make sense of the menacing promise on the wall.

Nate walked over and placed a tender hand on her shoulder. She jumped and looked up at him with frightened eyes. He somberly held up the bloody shard in the plastic bag.

"We are taking this to Detective Gray right now. I think it's safe to say that this guy knows exactly who you are."

CHAPTER 9

The police station was quiet when they walked in and Detective Gray came over quickly to greet them at the receptionist's station. Olivia took in his sloppy uniform, untucked and rumpled shirt and mussed up hair.

"Miss Miles, Mr. Freeman here called me a little while ago and filled me in on the troubles you have been having lately. Please do come in." He ushered them into a small conference room with a rectangular table and uncomfortable plastic seats.

Olivia and Nate sat down and after refusing the drinks Detective Gray offered them, Olivia ran through the recent events including the gunshot, the break in and vandalism of the wall at Nate's house. Nate slid him the baggie holding the broken glass and the detective quickly called a young officer over who grabbed it from him and disappeared into a room down the hall.

At the end of it all, Detective Gray shook his head in frustration and pressed his hands to his temple.

"Miss Miles, I do wish you had come to me immediately when this all had started. This guy is dangerous and if we had thought that there was any risk to you we would have put you into safe police custody immediately. We spoke to your lieutenant just yesterday and informed him that another body has been found in another fire on the other side of town."

Olivia played dumb, not wanting to give away any indication that she knew about the second body, "Another body? Is it the same guy?"

"We just determined this morning that the MO was the same so yeah," he replied, rubbing out the bags under his eyes, "Probably the same guy."

"Do you all have any leads yet?" Nate asked.

The detective sighed and crossed his arms, leaning back in his chair and staring blankly out the single glass window at the empty parking lot outside.

"We don't have an ID on the suspect yet, however we have two murders so far and all of them fit the profile. Both of the victims were younger women; both of them were killed by smoke inhalation and internal and external burns due to the fire he sets."

Olivia sucked in a shocked and disgusted breath.

"Smoke inhalation?" she whispered in realization, "So..."

The detective nodded solemnly, "He doesn't kill them beforehand. He lets the fire do that part."

"I just do not understand!" Olivia protested loudly, slamming her fists on the table as she stood up quickly and causing the detective to flinch by her outburst, "If I couldn't see a damn thing there is no way he could have seen who I was. I just don't understand how it is possible that he could have seen me!"

Nate tugged on her arm to get her to sit back down and she obliged, plopping back down ungracefully into the uncomfortable chair.

"Miss Miles," the detective continued, "whether or not you saw him, these incidents suggest that somehow he did see *you*. Maybe it was before you entered the building, maybe he hid in the trees after he ran off and waited to see who had almost caught him. Regardless, that is a *very* big problem. This guy is dangerous. He is a killer, and we need to make sure you do not become one of these women as well."

Olivia's head spun as covered her eyes with her hands. The edges of her vision began to darken and she rested her head on the cool table.

"Could I get some of that water now?" She asked weakly.

She felt Nate's hand rubbing her back soothingly as she tried to take deep breaths. A glass of water was soon handed to her and she sipped it slowly, trying to calm herself down.

"Are you okay Miss Miles?"

She looked up at Detective Gray and nodded.

"What do we do now?" She asked quietly, gripping the glass of water as if it were some sort of life preserver for her sanity.

"Twenty four hour police protection," he responded. "We can have someone stand guard at your home and we highly advise that you discontinue your work, at least until we can get a lead on this guy. It won't be easy for our men to protect you in the middle of you working a fire. And there's no guarantee that this guy won't set an intentional fire to lure you into a trap."

"I *cannot* miss work; the chief will have it in for me! He's just looking for a reason to fire me and this will give him just the ammo he needs to do it!" Olivia cried out in protest. She knew she sounded like a whiny child but right now her livelihood was at stake and this detective had no idea just how fine a line she walked at work with the chief always on her case. Nate turned to her and spoke softly.

"Miles, Chief Turner is out right now anyway...I'll talk to the lieutenant and let him know what's going on. Maybe by the time Turner gets better you'll be back and it won't be an issue."

The detective nodded in agreement. Before she could argue he continued.

"Miss Miles, we will contact the lieutenant and the chief as well to fill them in. This should not affect your status at your job. I know both of these men very well, and while I understand what a...challenge, it can be to work under the chief, I also know that he would never interfere in a police matter, or hold this against you."

She huffed with skepticism. If he only knew that the status at her job was touch and go every time she set foot in that station. Chief Turner only needed one reason to let her go and she was afraid at the rate things were going that this would be the reason.

"I think it is best that she continue to stay at my house with me as well." Nate chimed in.

"I highly disagree," Detective Gray told him, shaking his head "She is no safer at your place than she is at her own home, since he was able to track her there; and has already proven his ability to get in undetected. Not only that, but you would be unable to watch her at all times with your work schedule. And with one firefighter down, I'm sure your workload will be heavier than usual."

"That doesn't make any sense," Nate shook his head incredulously, "If he found her at my place, then he undoubtedly knows where she lives."

"Agreed," the detective acknowledged, "However, we will have police protection on her and a busy apartment complex would be a better place for her. Odds are this guy will have a harder time targeting her with witnesses around."

Nate crossed his arms and leaned back, "Fine, then I'll stay at her place when I'm not on shift."

"No you won't," Olivia told him quietly in protest.

He glared over at her, green eyes flashing. "Yes I will."

She didn't dare look at him, "No Nate, you

won't. Detective Gray already said I will have twenty-four hour police protection and that's all I need. I don't need you there babysitting me."

She knew he was mad. She could feel it in waves rolling off of him as he sat close to her, but she still kept her eyes focused on the stained wooden table in front of them. This was hard enough as it is, without feeling like she was interrupting his life too. And honestly her feelings about him recently were complicated and she needed a clear head.

"It's settled then," Detective Gray interrupted, "Miss Miles, an officer has already been sent out to Mr. Freeman's place and he should be finishing up his walk-through of the crime scene. You can pack what things you can salvage and head back to your apartment and we'll have the first shift officer stationed in the parking lot just outside your building. We'll send the shard of glass you brought in to be tested right away and will call you if we match any results to files in the system."

Olivia nodded and shook his hand, then walked out of the room quickly, trying not to look at Nate as she scurried out of the small police station, him hot on her heels.

As he drove them back to his house she fully expected a blowup but Nate kept surprisingly quiet. She couldn't understand why, and she didn't dare peek at him for fear that it might set him off.

It wasn't that she didn't want to be with

him. It was that she *did*, and that scared her. Because she knew she was setting her self up for disappointment. And as much as she felt for him she needed to distance herself to keep from falling for him and getting rejected. She also didn't need or want him feeling as though his own life was getting uprooted in the process or he could end up resenting her for it.

Back at the house, Olivia threw her torn up clothes and ruined makeup into a trash bag and packed what little was not destroyed back into her suitcase. She had to go through all of the yellow caution tape the officer had left behind and just doing that made her stomach uneasy.

She was just closing the latch on her suitcase when she looked up to see Nate watching her from the doorframe, his arms crossed over the white t-shirt that stretched across his muscles as he leaned against the doorjamb.

"Why are you doing this?" He asked suddenly, his green eyes watching her with a mixture of confusion and hurt.

"Doing what?" She responded softly, already knowing what he was referring to but she had been hoping to avoid the uncomfortable conversation.

He gestured around the room angrily.

"This! Why are you doing this? Why are you going back home instead of staying here with me where I can keep you safe?"

"You heard Detective Gray; I'm not safe at

your house..."

"You are safe with *me!*" He interrupted forcefully. "You don't even want me at your place when I'm off shift. It's like you don't trust me or something."

"Nate, I do trust you, I just can't..." she said slowly, pushing the tears back and avoiding his gaze for fear that the waterworks might start.

Nate crossed the room slowly, and tilted her chin up to look at him. She stared into his gorgeous green eyes and the tears she had desperately been trying to hold back started to fall.

And then he kissed her.

A sweet, soft kiss at first, tender and gentle, and in a matter of seconds his hands tangled in her hair and the kiss deepened, his tongue dancing in her mouth in earnest and wanting. Olivia let out a soft moan as she melted into him as he clung to her, his pelvis pushing against her stomach.

His hands skimmed her sides then lowered until they found her waist. She felt fingertips brushing the sensitive, bare skin under her shirt and in that moment it was as if a bucket of ice water had just been dumped over her. Olivia's eyes flew open and she frantically pushed Nate away. Her breathing quickened and her heart fluttered wildly as she stared at him with wide eyes and swollen lips.

He looked surprised at first, then embarrassed and then it was as if a light bulb had flashed over his head. This was a huge step for them and adding to the emotions of all the recent events he knew she had to be having an internal struggle.

"I-I…" She stammered, embarrassed herself at her reaction, suddenly realizing that the adrenaline of the day had her thoughts a complete mess in her head. She was excited, confused, scared, all at once and just couldn't seem to compose her brain at the moment.

She looked at her feet as her cheeks flamed, swiping at the drying tears staining her face. Nate reached out, stroked a tender finger down her cheek then gingerly kissed her forehead and she struggled to compose herself.

"When you are ready," he told her pointedly, "We are going to talk about this. Right now the important thing is to keep you safe. I wish you would reconsider me staying with you. I think I've shown you why I've wanted to protect you so much. I care for you Olivia, more than you could ever know."

"I thought…" she started, "I thought that you always saw me as a little sister. I never thought you were…attracted to me in that way."

As she said it her cheeks flamed at how stupid and childish she sounded. Butterflies danced in her stomach as her emotions churned with anxiety and hope at the same time.

He chuckled, running a hand through his hair again, a move Olivia was beginning to find extremely sexy, "And here I was afraid you would not want me. And then I was scared that I would lose you as a friend if I told you how I felt, so I kept quiet. But damn it, Liv, it was killing me; do you know how hard I wanted to pummel Dylan last night when I saw you too together?"

She grimaced, "I should not have said what I did, and I promise, I'm not remotely interested in Dylan...I was just, pissed off you know? I could tell it made you mad that you thought I was interested in him and I wanted to push you."

Nate shook his head and sighed, "I know. I shouldn't have been so angry at you, but I was worried, and now it looks like I have a good reason to be."

"Nate, I don't want you to pack up your life to babysit me, it's not fair to you."

Nate shook his head as he pulled her into his arms again, "I don't see it as babysitting, Olivia, I just want to keep you safe. I will do anything to keep this guy from getting to you. Please just let me stay with you."

He pulled back a few inches and turned his gaze on her, almost hypnotizing Olivia as she watched the swirls of jade and emerald plead with her. She nodded, knowing that she wouldn't trust anyone else to keep her safe and he leaned down to kiss her again.

He watched them from the shadows of the forest, through the shattered remains of the broken window. As he saw their lips lock, his fingernails dug painfully into the shards of glass that remained embedded in his palm from when he slammed his fist into that window to escape undetected. His groin stirred as the man's hands gripped her hair. "Soon," he thought, "soon those will be my hands." He slipped into the darkness of the trees as he chuckled softly.

CHAPTER 10

"Funny," Olivia said, turning on her apartment light as Nate walked past her and set her suitcase and his duffle bag on top of her kitchen table, "That whoever this is didn't break into my apartment and ransack that too."

"Well," Nate said, "you live upstairs. It's a lot harder to break a window when you have to shimmy up a drain pipe. Plus like the detective said, there are probably too many witnesses around here being that it's an apartment complex and all."

She nodded in agreement but something she couldn't quite put her finger on kept bothering her. She walked to her bedroom and started to look around at her unmade bed and tidy floors, searching for any little sign that something was out of place.

Nate came up behind her and placed a hand on her back as she walked over to her dresser and opened a drawer, rummaging through it.

"Is everything okay?" He asked.

Olivia shoved a few items of clothing aside, and satisfied, shut the cedar drawers. She ran her hand along the picture frames she had sitting on top of her dresser.

She shrugged, "I think so, just checking things. I just can't shake this feeling that something is off in here, but I don't see anything missing or out of place."

"Well I will be here all night to protect you, my fair maiden," Nate proclaimed, bowing before her in humor.

Olivia rolled her eyes, but her body quivered in excitement of the thought of Nate sleeping in her apartment overnight.

She cleared her throat nervously, "Um, why don't you take the bed and I'll sleep on the couch since you're taller?"

"I don't think so," he responded, "It's your apartment sweetheart, you take the bed, I can handle the couch. Or even that comfy recliner you always seem to be raving about."

Before she could protest, he walked off into the kitchen to unpack his things and she followed suit. As she put her clothes away she realized she would need to get Nate a spare key, just in case an emergency occurred. As she reached into the top drawer of her nightstand she felt empty space and her breath caught.

"Hey Nate?" She called out and he came jogging quickly into the room at her tone.

He walked over to where she stood and looked at her questioningly.

Olivia pointed to the empty drawer, "My

spare key. I always leave it in there and it's gone now."

Nate whipped his hand through the drawer and then got on his hands and knees to check the area around the nightstand. He came up empty-handed and shrugged as he got to his feet.

"Are you sure that's where you had it?"

She thought for a minute, "I think so; I mean I could have given it to Anne but I could have sworn she gave it back to me before she left on her vacation since she was planning to be gone for so long."

Nate shrugged again, not wanting to alarm her, "Well, maybe Anne still has it. You can check with her tomorrow, but I bet she just forgot to give it back or something."

"What's wrong?" he continued as he noticed the expression on her face change to one of confusion.

"I just..." she started. "I feel like a terrible friend, but I just realized that I haven't even spoken with Anne since our night out. I know Dylan got her home safe, and she texted me the day after but you know how she is. I figured she would want to know all about our little 'chat' at the bar that night. It's not like her to just patiently wait for gossip."

"That is a little odd," Nate agreed, "but she did just get back into town. Maybe she just got busy getting into the swing of things? I'm sure she'll reach out tomorrow or something. Why don't you send her a text if it'll make you feel better?"

Olivia nodded and did just that, feeling a little bit better when her friend immediately texted that she was busy getting situated after vacation but would want a brunch soon, but still a trace of doubt lingered in her mind. Maybe it was the stress of the situation with the fires and the killing but something nagged a little in the back of her mind that something was off with her friend. She waved Nate away so he wouldn't worry and he headed back to the living room while she finished putting her things away.

After unpacking, Olivia and Nate chowed down on some cans of soup she had in her pantry. She was embarrassed that she did not have more groceries but then again, she really had not had the time to go shopping lately.

After they ate, they watched a little bit of television and within an hour she had nodded off, her head resting comfortably on Nate's shoulder. He gently picked her up and carried her to her bed, tucking her in and kissing her lightly on the forehead before he settled onto the couch with a pillow and a sheet.

*   *   *

The next morning, Olivia woke up to the sun streaming through her window and she squinted into the brightness. She quickly smoothed her hair down before she got out of bed but stopped when she realized that Nate was on his shift that day and had probably already left for the morning. She peeked out of her window and relaxed a little as she spotted the white police car parked facing her building and the officer in the driver's seat, sipping coffee as he kept watch.

She went to the kitchen and poured herself a glass of orange juice, glancing over at her couch, where Nate had neatly folded his sheet and stacked it on top of the pillow she had lent to him that night. She sighed as she realized that he would be gone for two days now and she'd have to go at least one night sleeping by herself. As it was, she had slept like the dead last night, with the comfort of knowing Nate was just a few feet away.

Olivia finished her juice and took a quick shower, dressing in yoga pants and a pink shirt, and throwing her hair up into a bun. She went out on her balcony and spent an hour doing various yoga poses, letting it relax her and wipe away the stress of the past few weeks. After her workout, she sent a text to Anne about her key and her friend texted her back that she didn't think she had it but she was going to double check when she got home from work. Olivia hesitated to fill her friend in on everything that was going on but she went ahead and sent a quick message anyway.

I'm on 24 hr police protection. I'm fine but long story. Come by 2nite 2 catch up.

She was just making her bed when she heard the chime of the incoming text and smiled as she read the response.

Ok, um what?????!!!!!!!! Are you okay? OMG! Yes, I'll be there! With the wine AND the popcorn!

As her apartment was already clean, Olivia decided to sit down to pay some bills and surf the web a bit since she was stuck at home. She clicked on the local news website and immediately two images of young women flooded the screen. The first one she recognized as Jennifer Winthrop, the first young woman that had been killed. The other photo was very similar, a young woman with dark hair and eyes, both of them very beautiful. The second victim had now been identified as Chelsea Blake, the daughter of a well known business owner in Austin. She had been head cheerleader at the local high school and was supposed to be heading to a school in California to continue her cheerleading career in college. The article had few details about the murder but it did state that Chelsea had gone out to a party, and had simply never come home. The kids at the party stated that she had left on her own accord to walk home but no one saw anything after that and she had never arrived home.

Olivia flopped back in the chair and tried to push back the grief that threatened to overtake her. These girls were young, they would never get a chance to experience life and that thought cut through Olivia's heart as she stared at the beautiful brown eyes of the once full of life teen who had her whole life ahead of her.

As she sat there she began to get restless and she found herself scooping up the small white garbage bag in her kitchen trash can and heading outside with it. On impulse, she stopped at her refrigerator and grabbed a bottle of water. Once outside her door she stopped suddenly remembering something, then tucked the water under her arm and leaned down to undo the knot she had just tied on the bag. Olivia gently picked through the junk mail and trash and gingerly collected the note she had received earlier that week. She ran back inside her apartment and set it carefully down on the kitchen counter while she made the quick trip to the dumpster.

Olivia heaved the bag into the brown bin and then wiped her hands on her pants and headed over to the older man who was sitting in the cop car outside the apartment. He opened the door as she approached and introduced himself as Officer Williams. He seemed nice enough, slightly balding and a bit portly in the middle, but he had a gently smile and friendly blue eyes surrounded by laugh lines. She took a liking to him immediately and the anxiety that had been in her chest all day seemed to waver at the sight of him.

"Thank you so much for doing this," She told him apologetically as she handed him the bottle of cold water, "I know it's a pain to sit out here all day in this humidity."

He waved her off, "Just doing my job ma'am, beats chasing around gangbangers all day. Officer Davis will be relieving me tomorrow morning around this time so I'll make sure he comes up and introduces himself to you before I leave. Sure do appreciate the water."

Olivia thanked him again and told him about her friend Anne who would be arriving that evening. The last thing she wanted was for him to give her a hard time when she arrived, mainly because she didn't want Anne and her strong personality biting the nice man's head off. She waved goodbye as she headed back up to her apartment. She paced another twenty minutes in her kitchen and then finally decided to call Detective Gray, knowing it was necessary but also dreading the scolding she was surely to get for forgetting such a large piece of evidence.

After being transferred by the receptionist, his voice dripping with fatigue came on the line. She swallowed nervously and felt ashamed for brushing off what now seemed to be such an important piece of evidence.

"Yes Miss Miles, Sharon said you were calling with some more information?"

She hesitated, "Well, it's not exactly information, it's just..."

"Yes?" He prodded impatiently and she took a deep breath, knowing she should have mentioned this sooner.

Olivia explained the note as well as the phone calls that she had received. She still didn't know if the phone calls had just been a harmless prank but she figured she should mention it just in case. The detective sighed but gently told her that Officer Williams would come up to retrieve the note for evidence and that they would get a copy of her phone records to try to trace the phone call. She hung up feeling once again like she had been handling everything wrong. But then again, she never expected to be in this situation so who could blame her?

After Officer Williams stopped by to retrieve the note, Olivia spent the rest of the afternoon occupying herself with daytime television, a short nap and a finally settling down with a book she had started reading a few months before but had never gotten around to finishing.

The book was full of romance and she could not keep her thoughts from wandering to a certain brown haired, green eyed man. They still had not sat down and had a really serious talk about what had happened between them but she knew everything between them was about to change, hopefully for the better.

A knock on the door pulled her from her thoughts and a disheveled Anne stood in front of her when she opened it. She gave Olivia a comforting hug and wordlessly held up a chick flick and a bag of popcorn.

"You're a lifesaver," Olivia told her sincerely as Anne popped the movie into the DVD player then stuck the popcorn bag into the microwave.

"But of course," Anne remarked with a smile, "By the way, your super sweet bodyguard of a cop made me show him my ID. Don't worry, I gave him a pass since he's like, protecting you and all. Also, I looked everywhere for your key but I must have misplaced it."

Olivia watched Anne as she bounced around the kitchen, grabbing the bowl from a cupboard and humming. Her friend seemed to be in an awfully good mood and while Olivia was curious about the cause she was more concerned about the fact that the key was missing.

"Are you sure you had it Anne, I thought you had given it back to me before vacation?"

Anne poured the hot, steaming popcorn into a bowl, shook a ton of the powdered ranch flavoring on top of it and headed towards the living room.

"I'm pretty sure I had it, you know how bad I am at putting stuff where I can't find it." She replied carelessly.

"Are you sure..." Olivia continued.

"Uh, what is this?" Anne interrupted quickly, picking up the pillow and sheet that lay folded on the couch, "Sweetheart, are you in such a scary situation that you're sleeping on the couch now? Do I need to just move in for a while?"

"Um, no," Olivia replied uncomfortably, "Nate slept over last night."

Anne's eyes widened and she grabbed Olivia's hands and sat her down next to her on the couch, spilling popcorn onto the floor and cushions as she bounced with excitement.

"Tell me everything!" She squealed, popping a few kernels into her mouth.

Olivia sighed, "Well, we kissed..."

She jumped and covered her ears as Anne let out an ear-piercing shriek.

"I'm so sorry!" Anne apologized, clasping her hands together, "I'm just so excited for you guys! So how did it happen? Did you, you know? And was it good?"

"Whoa!" Olivia told her, holding up her hands to slow her friend down, "It just happened, no we didn't 'you know', and it was more than good, it was fantastic."

She sighed with contentment as she leaned back against the pillows.

Anne laughed with glee, "I knew it! I knew you liked him girl, I knew it all along! You can't hide things like that from your best friend."

Olivia shook her head but she could not stop herself from grinning.

"I think I knew it all along too," she agreed, "I just kept telling myself that he would never be interested so I pushed my feelings aside. But now that I know he is interested, I'm excited…and scared too."

"Of course you're scared honey," Anne replied with a romantic sigh, "But it is *so* worth it!"

Olivia knew her friend was right. She sighed and stared at the couple on the screen as they danced on the grass at an outdoor movie. Like a fairy tale. Between her parents' divorce when she was young and the mass of disastrous relationships her fellow firefighters had been through, Olivia had a hard time believing she would ever find a love like the one in the movie. But Nate was different. She could see herself loving him, but would he want her? Would it last? Their careers were the same and not without complications. They certainly could not show their relationship at work and how would they ever be able to handle kids with their schedules?

"So how are things going now that you're back?"

"Oh my word," she responded dramatically, "I am ready for my next trip already! I've already been looking at a cruise to Alaska, I need to add it to my repertoire for my clients anyway. It's hard to be here sometimes, I just need more excitement in my life, you know?"

Olivia grinned and raised an eyebrow at her friend.

"Maybe you just need an exciting *man* in your life."

"What like the guy from the bar?" She snorted, "I didn't even go home with the jerk, and Dylan drove me home. Apparently he didn't score either."

"Well what about Erik?"

"What about Erik?" Anne replied suspiciously, stuffing a handful of buttery popcorn into her mouth, and Olivia noticed a little red creeping into her friend's cheeks. Any time Anne was back in town and Erik was around they would trade flirtatious compliments but both were such free spirits that they never acted on it.

Olivia simply shrugged and turned back to the movie. She sat there a while in silence while she let Anne mull it over. She knew her friend too well and was not surprised when she heard her resounding sigh.

"I know, I know," Anne answered, "Erik's hot, and he's just my type, fun and flirty and, well, all *man*! But Liv, I don't know if I want to keep playing the field, sleeping with a different guy every week and not settling down. I think I might be ready for an actual relationship, you know? And Erik has a new woman almost every time I see him. While I like the flexibility of being with someone who has the same carefree attitude towards life I also don't want to sell myself short, you know?"

Olivia did know. She knew even better now that she knew she had a chance with Nate. While she definitely did not understand the sleeping around part, she understood being alone and not having someone to come home to, someone to share holidays and feelings with. And she for sure understood the fear of becoming connected with someone only to have them flitter off the second they change their mind.

Anne and Olivia remained quiet after that while they finished the movie and ate their way through the popcorn, and finally Anne left for the evening and Olivia locked the door securely behind her, glancing out the peephole at her friend's retreating back. She threw the excess kernels of corn in the trash and began to set the bowl down on the counter. Her ringtone startled her and she knocked the bowl over onto the floor, scolding herself for being so jumpy.

"Olivia, its Nate, are you awake?" His voice was urgent and hard to understand through the screaming of the sirens in the background.

"Nate?" Olivia repeated, "Aren't you working? Yeah I'm still awake, what's wrong?"

"I needed to call you, we are headed out to a fire..."

Olivia waited for him to continue. She wasn't sure what the big deal was but she knew Nate and his tone said that something was wrong. Had they found another body?

"Liv," he continued gently, and she could tell he was trying to speak in a calm tone," The fire is at your dad's house."

Olivia froze and for a second she couldn't hear the words of comfort and reassurance coming through the other end of the phone line. She shook her head and tried to focus.

"I'm coming over," she told Nate, and hung up swiftly before he could answer. She quickly threw a hoodie on over her small pink yoga top, zipped it up, then dashed out the door and threw herself down the stairs, ignoring the incessant ringing of her phone in her pocket.

"Miss Miles, is everything okay?" The kind police officer quickly got out of his car, weapon drawn as he watched the young woman scurrying towards him. His eyes searched the area behind her for signs of trouble.

"Fire," Olivia breathed out frantically, "At my dad's house...please..."

He nodded in understanding and motioned for her to get into his patrol car. She clambered into the passenger seat, barely remembering to buckle her seatbelt as she rattled off his address, and they sped off, lights flashing towards her father's house. The drive only took fifteen minutes but it had felt like hours to Olivia and by the time they reached her father's neighborhood, she had chewed one fingernail down to almost a nub.

She watched the billow of black smoke coming from a few streets away and closed her eyes in silent prayer as Officer Williams turned and headed in the direction of the house. As they approached, Olivia saw the familiar sight of fire trucks, lights flashing, and streams of water pointed at the home and her stomach dropped.

Before Officer Williams could even stop the car, Olivia unbuckled her seat belt and threw herself out onto the sidewalk, scrambling to reach the ambulance sitting in front of the burning structure. She almost cried when she spotted her father standing outside of the ambulance, wrapped in a gray towel and taking occasional breaths from an oxygen mask that Nate was holding for him.

"Daddy?!!" She cried out as she threw herself at him in relief and both of them almost fell over with the impact.

"What are you doing here sweetie?" he asked her with concern, as she just about sobbed with relief.

She looked up at him incredulously, her arms still wrapped around him tightly.

"Are you kidding? Dad, why wouldn't I be here? Are you okay? Why didn't you call me?"

He pulled back and gave her a stern look, "Honey, Nate here filled me in on the other murders and he told me about the break-in. It's not safe for you out in the open, you should be safe at home."

His gaze swung over to Nate accusingly, and the fireman raised his hands in defense.

"I'm sorry sir, but you know Olivia would have never forgiven me if I hadn't called you. And she has police protection, otherwise there was no way I would have let her run over here."

"Please dad," Olivia pleaded, gesturing to the uniformed man standing a few feet away, "Officer Williams is with me so I'll be fine. Is Darcy okay?"

"Darcy broke her arm in all of the chaos," he told her with a sigh, "She's in the ambulance resting right now after all the meds they have given her but she is going to be okay. They are going to take her to the hospital soon to do some x-rays and get a cast on her."

Olivia glanced into the open doors of the ambulance and saw that Darcy was indeed quietly sleeping, her arm wrapped in a white sling, soot marks marring her cheeks, and her heart melted.

She felt relieved that Darcy was okay but she felt awful that she was in pain.

She turned to look at her father's home and watched as the burning pieces of wood collapsed into black heaps on the concrete foundation while strong jets of water chiseled away at the flames. Mrs. White and her husband stood out on the sidewalk, a security precaution in case the fire jumped, and watched in shock. Olivia put her hand on her father's shoulder in comfort.

"Dad, I am so sorry about the house."

"It's alright," he responded, "It can be rebuilt of course, just lucky that Darcy and I made it out alive, you know? Can't say the same about your peach pie."

He chuckled nervously and she knew he was trying to use humor to distract him from what could have happened to Darcy and to him.

"What happened?" Olivia prodded gently.

He shrugged in response, "I don't really know. I'm thinking maybe it was some old wiring or something. You know that house is almost a hundred years old, I should have had the wiring checked..."

Olivia shook her head quickly, "This wasn't your fault dad, and you know that."

He turned to look at her, his tired eyes older than she remembered and full of remorse and guilt. Her heart tugged in her chest.

"I'm a retired firefighter, I should know better..." Her father looked down and shook his head, "Anyhow, we were asleep and I began to smell smoke. I thought it was strange that none of the smoke detectors had gone off and when I got out of bed, I saw that our door was closed and smoke was creeping into the room through the crack at the bottom."

He took a deep breath and continued.

"I woke Darcy and the smoke moved so fast, the room was filling up, so I pulled her down onto the floor with me and we crawled to the window. I couldn't get it open, that old window has been stuck for years, and I hadn't gotten around to fixing it so I had to leave Darcy by the window while I grabbed a chair to break it. I broke the window open and she went first but she landed wrong on her arm. I jumped out afterwards and by then 61 was showing up. Nate over there stayed with us and helped with Darcy's arm until the ambulance showed up."

Her father gestured in appreciation at Nate who had just jumped backed in with the other firefighters to help spray down the house. His eyes were glowing like emeralds through the clear material of his face mask as he pointed an open nozzle towards the remnants of the flames that were now nearly out. Her heart fluttered and she felt a pang that stabbed straight through her chest.

She turned back to her dad who was currently speaking with the driver of the ambulance.

"Hey sweetheart," he turned back to her and

removed the blanket from his shoulders, "They're going to take Darcy in now, so I'm going to go with them. You should get home and sleep hon; it's not safe out here in the open."

"I should be with you and Darcy," Olivia countered, shaking her head.

"No baby," her father shook his head, "There is no need. I will be there with her and Darcy will understand. She knows the situation as well and she would feel better if she knew you were being kept safe."

Officer Williams stepped forward from his position a few feet away and nodded in agreement. Olivia hugged her father and with a last look at Nate, who still had his attention turned to the fire, she followed the officer to his car.

He watched from a distance, hidden in the darkness of his car. Watched him scramble to put out the fire he started. He didn't intend to kill the man and woman, just to scare them. Killing would come later. He watched her walk to the police car with her "escort". The throb inside of him ached to get to her now. He needed to act soon, he thought. He would too, his plans were almost finished. He hunkered down as the police vehicle cruised by and then quietly started the engine and left his hiding place.

CHAPTER 11

The clanging of the fire alarm woke Olivia up from a dreamless sleep and for a second she was disoriented, thinking she was at the station and a call had come in. She glanced around the still dark room and quickly pulled a robe on over her shorts and tank top and slipped on some flip flops, grabbing her purse as she rushed out of the apartment and quickly locking the door behind her. As she descended the stairs she collided with Officer Williams who also looked as if he had been sleeping.

"Are you alright?" he hollered over the sound of the alarm and she nodded as they retreated down the steps to the parking lot. A crowd had already gathered, most of them yawning and still in their pajamas. Olivia sniffed the air and looked around but she saw no cause for the fire alarm.

"Come with me," Officer Williams ordered her. She obeyed and they headed to the front office where the office manager was just arriving to shut off the loud device. As the older woman pushed the handle back into place she waved a hand at Officer

Williams and Olivia.

"Some punks must have pulled it, there's no fire," the gray-haired lady declared, rolling her eyes in annoyance, "This isn't the first time."

"Mind if I take a look around?" The officer asked as he pulled a flashlight out and began to walk around the building.

"Be my guest," she responded, waving him on and heading to the parking lot to inform the residents of the false alarm.

Olivia stayed behind Officer Williams as he made a circle around the building, checking the windows and doors. Satisfied everything was locked and looked safe, he slid his flashlight back into his pocket and shrugged.

"Looks like your landlady was right," he stated, "Let's get you back to your apartment."

Olivia obliged and they headed back up the stairs of the building to her place. As they approached her door was open and Officer Williams gave her a questioning look.

"I locked that earlier," she declared nervously, as her hands started to tremble. In response, Officer Williams motioned quietly for her to stay outside of the doorway and he drew his gun from his holster as he entered the apartment.

Olivia stood outside, her hands clasped in fear as her eyes darted to the dark empty stairwell on the other side of her. It seemed as though ages had passed when she finally heard the officer's voice from the doorway, startling her and causing her heart to race.

"Miss Miles, I need you to follow me quickly to my vehicle, can you do that?" He asked her intently, his face pale.

"What is it?" She asked pointedly, afraid of his answer.

He glanced back into the apartment, "We need to get you to a safe place *now*."

It was then that Olivia saw a slight smear of blood on the door frame and without thinking she rushed past the officer to peer into her apartment, ignoring his shouts behind her. At first she was confused as to what she was seeing. Black tufts and red masses littered her kitchen counter as a sickening smell hit her nostrils, causing her to gag on reflex. Something glinted in the middle of the unknown debris and as she stepped closer and realized what it was her mouth opened into a silent scream.

* * *

"Olivia!"

Her eyes welled up yet again as she heard Nate calling her name. Fresh tears spilled down her cheeks when she saw his tall frame running down the linoleum-floored hall towards her.

She flew into his arms and sobbed as he kissed her hair in an attempt to console her. Her tears soaked into his black t-shirt and she clutched the fabric until her knuckles had ached and turned white. She inhaled the smoky masculine scent that imbedded itself in his shirt and began to cry even harder.

"I'm so sorry you saw that," he whispered.

The image burned on her brain of hair, internal organs and blood on her kitchen table, all surrounding a gold Fire Chief badge emblazoned with the name "Turner" on it, caused her to shudder and she clung to Nate to keep from completely losing control.

She didn't know how long they stood there, him whispering kind words while she cried until her eyes dried up and she could cry no more tears.

"It's my fault," she whispered between sniffles.

Nate pulled back from her in response and gripped her face in both hands, forcing her to look at him. His eyes blazed with anger.

"Olivia this is no one's fault, no one but the evil person who is doing this. Don't you *ever* think that, do you hear me?"

His green eyes burned intensely into her hazel ones and she nodded in reply, suddenly exhausted. Her knees began to buckle and he quickly led her over to the row of chairs against the wall.

"You sit right here, okay? I'm going to go talk to the detective." Nate gently lowered her down onto a plastic chair and headed towards the group of men who were standing a few feet away. After Detective Gray had taken her statement, a few men in black suits had shown up and they and the detective had been speaking frantically in hushed tones ever since they arrived at the police station.

Flashes of blood and torn flesh flew through her vision in a sick montage and Olivia squeezed her eyes tightly and shook her head, trying to forget the image of the dead carcass that had adorned her table top. As she stared at the linoleum floor, her vision blurred again and she swiped at her wet lashes frantically to stop the flow of tears that threatened to restart.

She heard a noise and Olivia looked up to see Detective Gray and Nate walking her way with a sympathetic look on his face. The detective stopped just in front of her and motioned to the nearby office that the men in suits had just stepped into.

"Miss Miles," he began soothingly, "The FBI is now involved in this case and they would like to speak to you if that is okay. Will you be able to talk with them now?"

Olivia nodded numbly as Nate took her arm and helped her to her feet, guiding her to the small office where the two agents stood expectantly.

One of the agents stopped them at the door and gave Nate a hard glare.

"We need to speak with her alone please," he ordered Nate and Olivia could feel the hand around her elbow tense with anger.

"It's okay Nate," she assured him strongly, patting his hand, "I will be okay, just wait for me here with Detective Gray okay?"

Nate hesitated but resolutely dropped his

arm and headed toward the chairs obligingly as Olivia followed the big burly agent into the room.

"Miss Miles," the other agent smiled at her as she entered and motioned for her to have a seat. "We just have a few questions about some recent events if that is okay."

Olivia nodded in response as she sat down in the black folding chair, her legs shaking with adrenaline as she did so.

The interrogation was very similar to the detective's after the break-in incident at Nate's house. Olivia had to recount all of the events over the past week; the fire, the prank calls, the note, the break in and finally, the remnants of Chief Turner found on her kitchen table. When she went over what she had walked into at her apartment she had to take deep breaths to staunch the waves of nausea that threatened to overtake her.

The agents were quiet the whole time, simply listening and taking notes as she spoke. They asked a few questions but mainly it seemed as though they had most of the information already and were just getting her to reiterate the events. Olivia knew that the detective must have already gone over everything with them earlier.

"Thank you Miss Miles," the nicer agent told her as he headed over to the door and opened it for her, "Please wait out in the hall for a few minutes, we would like to speak to Detective Gray again."

Olivia nodded and did as they asked, taking a seat next to Nate and settling into the arm he offered her. Exhausted from the early morning's events, she closed her eyes and tried to block out visions of blood and death.

A few minutes later, she stirred as Nate's strong arms lifted her and carried her like a child to a black suburban parked out front. She snuggled into his warmth as he settled into the backseat with her and the two men in suits settled into the front seats.

"What's going on? Where are we going?" she mumbled wearily as they started to drive.

"It's okay," he whispered, his lips brushing her ear. "The FBI agents are taking us to a safe house. They don't think it's safe for you to stay in town anymore. They want to keep you out of public view until they find this guy. Supposedly some agents are coming in tonight to start following leads with the detective."

"What about my family? My dad? Darcy?"

"Shh," he assured her, "Don't you worry about that. They have an agent staying with your dad and Darcy who are staying at a hotel in town. He'll keep them safe."

Olivia sat up a bit and reached into her purse, "I need to text Anne, and Daddy. With everything going on they'll be worried if I just up and disappear..."

As she pulled her cell out of her purse Nate's hands closed over it, "Sorry hon, I know that it sucks but they said no calls unless it is an emergency. We don't want this guy to track us. Besides I already sent a text to them from my phone letting them know the situation, well as much of it as I could with the agents' permission."

"Oh, right, thanks." Olivia mumbled unhappily as she shut the phone with a click and slipped it into the front inside pocket of the terry cloth robe she still had on from being woken up early in the morning.

"I feel just awful Nate," she said, looking up at him, "I mean, I *hated* the chief, but I would have never wished death on him. I can't help feeling like this is somehow my fault. Or that because I hate him this happened."

"Liv," Nate stroked her cheek with his fingers, "You are not responsible for his death. This sicko is and that is all there is to it. You need to stop beating yourself up about it, there was absolutely nothing you could have done."

He rested his chin on her head, "It was awful Liv. The lieutenant got a call at the station from Detective Gray and the first thing I thought of was that something had happened to you. I think I had a momentary heart attack at that point. I don't know what I would do if I lost you."

He hugged his arms tighter around her and Olivia's heart fluttered at the thought that Nate cared so deeply about her. She sat there, wrapped safe in his arms and immediately decided that she needed to stop being so selfish. She took a deep breath and then pulled away from Nate and turned to face him.

"Nate, I need to tell you the truth...when I pushed you away...I just, I'm sorry for..."

She hesitated and glanced again at the two feds in the front seat remembering that they were not quite alone and Nate shushed her.

"We'll talk later; right now you need to rest." He pulled her back to him and she snuggled into his side and fell into a deep sleep.

CHAPTER 12

As the suburban pulled up to a heavily wooded home somewhere in Louisiana, Olivia awoke with a jolt. She quickly rubbed the sleep from her eyes as one of the agents opened the rear passenger door and Nate slid out. He turned, offering her hand and helped her out of the vehicle and all together they approached the small, one story home. It was simple, with few windows and no visible neighbors. Tall trees and swampy areas surrounded the plain structure and a single gravel path allowed for one car to maneuver up to the house. Beyond the gravel road she could see the path turn to dirt and extend a ways into the woods but could not tell how far it stretched. A small building stood off to one side, almost a bit like a shack but made of concrete and less run down. Possibly a guard post?

Olivia looked around as the agents and Nate lugged the bags from the back of the vehicle up the rickety wooden porch steps that led to the front door. The air was humid, and the night eerily quiet, save for a few crickets and cicadas chirping in the distance. Mr. Nice Agent, as Olivia had decided to nickname him, was a short, but fit older man with wire-rimmed glasses and steel-blue eyes. She watched as he threw a few black duffle bags into the small wooden building that stood off to the side, answering her question about the possible identity of that structure.

She held her breath as the taller agent (Mr. Grump) unlocked the front door and released it into the damp air as it swung open with a very loud creak. Nate ushered her in with his free hand and she entered the home, immediately inhaling the scent of cleaning solution.

Mr. Grump turned on a lamp in the living room and Olivia looked around, happy to see that it was a fully furnished and indeed very clean space. A slight bit of dust lingered from an obvious lack of use, but it was charming and warm just the same. It was small, with what looked like just one bedroom and bathroom, living space and a small kitchen. Simple, pleasant and secluded.

After setting the bags on the kitchen counter the scowling agent formally introduced himself to Olivia as Agent Sims. She took in his thick-muscled form along with the no-nonsense look of his dark eyes and she blew out a breath she hadn't even realized she was holding, feeling a little better protected and glad that he was on her side. She took his hand and subsequently shook the hand of the other agent, Agent Brockman, as he glided back in from outside and locked the door behind him.

"We are here to protect you Miss Miles," Agent Sims told her in an all business tone, "If you need anything at all please use this disposable cell to contact us."

She took the small black phone that he held in his beefy hand and absently scrolled through the short contact list.

"A few federal contacts are listed there, along with our numbers," he answered her unspoken question. "Any little sign of trouble, call us and we will have someone here in a few seconds."

She nodded in response, pocketing the phone.

"One of us will always be standing guard, typically walking around the perimeter, making sure there is no threat to you or us," Agent Brockman told her. His voice was gentler, more fatherly, and Olivia figured the two had not been paired together on accident.

"This is a heavily wooded area," Nate spoke up, crossing his arms over his chest, "How can you be positive that your suspect isn't already lurking in the woods or that he hasn't followed us here?"

"Mr. Freeman," Agent Sims countered defensively, "You have two of the best highly trained federal agents at your disposal. *Nothing* is going to get to Miss Miles under our watch, I can guarantee you that. While one of us scouts the perimeter, the other will be setup in the building next door where we have surveillance cameras covering the area."

That answered the question about the guard post and Olivia exhaled a slight breath of relief. It sounded like these guys really had all the bases covered to keep them safe.

"We also have no reason to believe that the suspect is aware of Miss Miles's location," Agent Brockman interjected, "Agent Sims did an excellent job of taking an indirect route to this area, one that the suspect would have not been able to follow had he even seen us take off from the hospital."

Nate did not look entirely convinced but he shrugged, and Olivia realized in the lamp light just how fatigued he looked. Soot still streaked his handsome face and his eyes drooped as though he could pass out on the spot.

The agents did a final walkthrough of the interior of the cabin and then headed out to their post, instructing Nate to lock the front door behind them.

Olivia studied his profile as he peered out of the dark curtains into the quiet night and admired the way the shadows danced across his chiseled jaw and cheekbones. The shirt he wore was fitted and the hard planes of his chest just begged to be touched. His green eyes stared intensely through the glass and his soft lips pursed in concern. He turned and caught her staring and frowned curiously.

"Are you okay Liv?" He asked her gently, his

brow furrowed with worry.

She approached him slowly. Timidly and trembling she stood on her tiptoes, clasping his strong arms for leverage and reveled in the smooth firmness of his strong biceps. Her lips pressed softly to his and a tremor went through her body. He froze in surprise, then quickly returned the kiss and wrapped his arms around her as she slid her tongue lightly across his lips. Olivia clung to him as desire took over and she kissed him passionately, as if she would never be able to kiss him again. She formed her body to his and he groaned in agony as his hardness pressed against her stomach. It was easy to see that he wanted her and it made her want him even more. She let out a small moan as their mouths intertwined. Her hands ran down his back pulling at him and gripping at his shirt, wanting him closer.

Abruptly, Nate pulled away and backed up, placing some distance between them, his chest heaving with each breath and she swallowed and tried not to look as rejected as she felt.

"Liv, sweetheart," he said gently and carefully, "I know you have been through a lot today. I don't want to take advantage of you being in such a fragile state."

Olivia stepped towards him but he sidestepped her, increasing the space between them with his long stride. She shook her head roughly and stared at him pleadingly.

"Nate, please," she argued, "This has nothing

to do with anything that's been going on. Do you really think this isn't something I haven't been wanting for a very long time?"

Olivia looked down at her feet, color flooding her cheeks as she spoke softly, "I've always wanted you."

She could smell the slight scent of smoke as it got closer and before she knew it Nate was in front of her again, his hands gripping her chin and lifting her face to his.

"Ditto," he said softly and his lips once again found hers, hungry and passionate as years of repressed attraction slammed into them both in a matter of seconds. His fingers fumbled with the knot at her waist and the robe fell to the floor in a heap.

Nate lifted her up and she wrapped her legs around him as he carried her swiftly through the doorway of the lone bedroom. He laid her down on the king size bed with the plain taupe comforter and slipped his shirt off. Olivia got up on her knees and as he tossed the shirt on the floor she greedily kissed the surface of his hard abs. He slid her robe quickly down her shoulders and threw it onto the wood floor in a heap. Moaning slightly he pulled her face to him and covered her mouth greedily with his. His hands trailed up the sides of her legs as he gently laid her back down on the bed and goosebumps formed where his fingertips caressed. Nate slid his hands under the waistbands of her shorts and looked up at her questioningly already knowing the answer but she nodded anyway. Slowly he slid her shorts down to her ankles and he trailed gentle kisses down the smooth silk of her legs.

Olivia boldly pulled her tank top up and over her head, exposing her firm breasts and she whimpered as he crawled over her and kissed the tender flesh. She reached down and unbuckled his belt, letting him lift up to slide his pants off and then his boxers, freeing himself. The heat between her legs felt like fire and she almost cried when he cupped his hand between her legs and rubbed her through her panties. She bucked against his hand and he uttered a primal growl, quickly ripping the lacy material down her thighs.

He nipped at her neck as his fingers rubbed and then slowly entered her. She cried out and lifted her hips, writhing on his hand and wanting more, needing more. She reached down and gently took hold of him, stroking him and feeling every ridge, memorizing him with her fingertips.

He looked down at her, "You are so beautiful," he murmured as he positioned himself between her legs and carefully nudged between them with his hardness.

Nate stared deep into her eyes and she closed her eyes in pleasure as he slowly pushed into her, filling and stretching her so that she cried out.

"Are you okay?" he asked, stopping.

She nodded and after a few agonizing

seconds, she reached up and kissed him, gripping and pulling his hips, letting him know that she was ready for more. He finally pushed all the way in and after a few slow strokes he began going faster, making her squeal and scream with desire as he drove into her over and over again. She dug her nails into his back as pleasure took over and she screamed as she bucked against him, a wave of ecstasy overcoming her body. He probed her mouth with his tongue and she cried out in pleasure into his mouth. As her orgasm subsided, he couldn't hold back any longer. Thrusting harder and deeper he let out a guttural moan and then emptied himself into her as she clung to him in desire.

When they had finally begun to catch their breath, Nate turned onto his side, pulling Olivia with him and stroking her hair as she nuzzled into the crook of his neck. Kissing her forehead, he trailed his hand down her neck to her collarbone.

"I meant it," he said.

"Meant what?" She asked him sleepily.

"You are beautiful. You are the most beautiful woman in the world. I've wanted you ever since you came back from college."

She leaned up on one elbow, blinking in surprise, "Seriously?"

"Of course I have, why would I not? You're amazing. Smart, funny, full of life and energy, you are a passionate and kick ass firefighter and you have a way about you that works me just right, in more ways than one." He smiled impishly, his green eyes sparkling.

She pushed against him playfully, "I'm pretty sure you were working me, not the other way around."

He chuckled, ruffling her hair, "Either way, this was a long time coming."

Olivia smiled and leaned over to pick up his black t-shirt from the floor and tug it over her head, inhaling the smoke residue that emitted from the soft cotton fabric. She crawled back under the covers facing him, tenderly stroking his chiseled jaw with her fingertips.

"I love you Olivia Miles," he told her as he stared into pools of topaz.

"Ditto," she whispered.

She opened her eyes and suddenly she was in her own bed in her apartment. Her hand drifted to the sheets next to her and it was cold and empty.

"Nate?" She called out into the darkness. She listened quietly and heard a noise in the kitchen. Carefully she slipped out of bed and headed towards the sound.

"Nate is that you?"

She rounded the corner and as she did, she saw flames surrounding her front door and traveling along the old carpet into her living room.

"Nate!" She screamed and dashed to her pantry to grab her extinguisher. She picked up the small red device and went to aim it at the fire but nothing happened when she pulled the lever. Olivia

shook the extinguisher rapidly and realized to her dismay that it was empty. She tossed it aside and stared at the engulfed front door, her only way out.

She frantically looked around and her heartbeat rose as she realized that the room was beginning to fill up with smoke. Olivia ran over to her balcony and flung open the glass door, sprinting out into the fresh air. She looked down and suddenly her apartment seemed ten stories high. There was no way she would survive that jump.

Thinking that she could use her bed sheet and tie it to her balcony to climb down, she ran back into the fire-filled apartment and coughed and sputtered as her eyes stung with the smoke.

"Olivia!" A voice screamed out and as she looked towards her kitchen, she saw Nate on the table, laying where the chief's blood and organs had been, blood pouring from his own stomach and spilling over the counter and onto the floor.

"Nate!" She screamed in horror.

"Shhh, Liv, I'm here, I'm here," Nate coaxed her as she rocked and cried in his arms. She sobbed loudly as the image in her head refused to dilute and she clung to him as if she would never see him again.

When she had cried enough, Olivia peered up tearfully at the man holding her. They were back at the cabin, he was safe, there was no fire, they were both okay for now.

"Nate, you were...I was...there was a fire... and you were on the table...not Turner..." She stammered as she struggled to hold back more tears.

"It's okay baby," he comforted her, stroking her hair and kissing her forehead, "We're okay, it was just a bad dream. Just the adrenaline and everything, it's all coming back to you right now."

"When will it all be over? Why is this happening to me?" She asked him woefully, looking up at him with big hazel eyes. His heart broke for her.

"I don't know," he answered honestly. "When they get this guy, which they will, the nightmares will eventually stop. When you know that you are perfectly safe and that without a doubt none of this is your fault, they will stop."

"Do you ever have nightmares?" She asked him, as she clung to his hand desperately, "About, you know, that family?"

Nate looked down at their entwined fingers and sighed.

"I used to a lot," he said, "Especially when I started to fight fires. I would worry that one day I would be sent out to a fire and there would be someone trapped in there and I would be too late."

He turned Olivia to face him and stared into her eyes.

"When I was a rookie, we went to a fire, a bad one, and when we got there, there were people trapped inside. Your dad was in charge and he led me and another guy in there and we saved everyone, we got them all out. And I remember afterwards, a little kid from the house was screaming about his dog. We never found a dog until after the fire had been put out."

Nate hung his head, "I felt awful. I kept seeing that poor kid's face and thinking that I should have known, I should have found that dog! It wasn't a person, no, but it was a member of their family and we *missed* it."

"I remember when we got back to the station that immediately your dad knew something was wrong. He didn't have to ask and I didn't have to say anything but he's got a real good read on people and he knew that I was upset. He just looked at me as I hung up my gear and I will never forget what he said."

Olivia looked at Nate expectantly.

"He told me, 'Son, it's our job to put out the fires, but we don't set them. We do what we can do but ultimately it's in God's hands. We saved a family today and they may mourn their pet now, but that will heal. They will never, however, forget the fact that we risked our lives to save them, and we did.'"

"I realized that I can't beat myself up every time I can't save someone or something. I can't be mad at myself I can only blame the person or thing that set the fire. That's when I stopped having the nightmares."

He pulled Olivia back into his arms and hugged her tight.

"You need to realize that none of this is your

fault. Yes, you are involved but you need to blame this sick bastard that is killing people, not yourself. You were just at the wrong place at the wrong time."

He kissed her deeply then snuggled back under the blankets with her, tucking her into his side. She leaned her head into the curve of his neck and inhaled the delicious scent as she shut her eyes and reveled in his comfort.

"Now go back to sleep and dream about sailing or something," he told her and she chuckled sleepily as she obliged.

CHAPTER 13

The next morning Olivia woke to empty sheets and the smell of bacon and eggs coming from the kitchen. She could hear Agent Brockman and Nate talking so she decided to take a quick shower. One of the bags that they had brought in the night before was on the nightstand and as she pawed through it she was relieved to see it contained several articles of clothing. She grabbed a pair of jeans and a red t-shirt and padded over to the small bathroom. As she scrubbed and rinsed she smiled and blushed at the memories of the evening before. Her fingertips gliding over her body only reminded her of Nate's hands on her the night before. Humming to herself she dried her hair quickly then got dressed and headed to the kitchen for breakfast.

"Morning Miss Miles," Agent Brockman smiled warmly at her as he sat at the kitchen counter, sipping coffee from a plain white mug, "Did you sleep well?"

She froze in place and glanced quickly at Nate, her cheeks reddening, but his back was turned as he pushed some scrambled eggs around in a pan.

"I slept great, thank you," she replied to the agent, embarrassed once she realized his question was not an implication of guilt. She could have sworn she could see Nate's cheeks lift into a smile from behind.

She sat on one of the tall wooden chairs as well and smiled shyly at Nate as he set a plate of food in front of her. He grinned, eyes twinkling, and his dimple causing her heart to flutter. She shook her head to clear her thoughts as she dug into her breakfast.

"Where's Agent Sims?" Olivia asked as she took a sip of orange juice from the glass Nate had set in front of her and greedily took a bite of the hot eggs.

"Walking the perimeter," Agent Brockman replied between bites of bacon.

"Any leads yet that connect this guy to all of the other murders or why he's going after Olivia?" Nate asked as he sat down with his own plate of heaping eggs.

"We have found a small sample of DNA at one of the previous crime scenes that we have just sent off to get analyzed, but unless it matches someone in the database, we don't have too much to go off of."

The agent sipped his coffee thoughtfully, "As for why he hasn't tried to directly attack Miss Miles and why he would choose to leave a body at her apartment, we are not sure. He could simply be toying with her. A lot of these serial killers consider themselves artists and tend to try to get "creative" in their methods."

Olivia shuddered and Nate, noticing she was uncomfortable, changed the subject to what the plans were for her safety.

"We will be here twenty-four-seven, and one of us will always be on guard outside. If you all need anything, groceries and the like, let us know and we have agents that can make drop offs for us on a regular basis. The most important thing is that you do not make personal calls and that you don't leave the house."

They all ate in silence for the next few minutes and Olivia was grateful for the food that she realized her stomach had been badly missing. When was the last time she had eaten? She couldn't even remember and was extremely grateful when Nate kept slipping slices of extra toast and bacon onto her plate.

"Well," Agent Brockman stated when they were all wrapping up with breakfast. He wiped his mouth with a napkin and stood up, "I better go relieve Agent Sims so that he can partake in this wonderful breakfast. Thank you again Mr. Freeman."

Nate gave him a small salute with his fork as he took his plate over to the sink and dropped it in, giving it a quick rinse with the tap. Olivia watched as Agent Brockman shrugged into his black suit jacket and headed out the front door, closing it carefully behind him. She peeked over at Nate cautiously. She blushed as she realized he was leaning back against the sink and staring right at her and the coloring in her cheeks deepened as he winked at her.

"I'm, um…" she stammered, unsure of what to say. Nate smiled and stood up suddenly, walked over to her and kissed her gently on the forehead.

"Morning," he told her sweetly as he grabbed the two empty plates on the counter and tossed them into the sink as well. As if on cue, the other agent walked in with his signature scowl, the complete opposite of the agent that had just walked out. It wasn't hard to tell who of the two agents might play "good cop" or "bad cop" when these guys had to interrogate people.

"Grub?" Nate asked Agent Sims simply and the agent nodded as he took a seat.

"I'm uh, going to go unpack us a little…" Olivia stammered at the two men as she hurried out of the room and back to the bedroom. She had to admit, she was grateful that the federal agents were here for her protection but it also made the "morning after" with Nate a bit awkward. She started to pull some clothing out of the first bag on the bed and folded the various items neatly, slipping them into the single cedar chest in the room. She could hear Nate and Agent Sims talking and she knew now that she was out of the picture, it was most likely more talk about the fires and the victims and what this killer could be capable of.

As she tossed a few balls of socks into the top drawer of the chest, a loud explosion suddenly rocked the house and Olivia crumpled to the ground, covering her head in reflex as the walls shook around her. She heard shouts and loud footsteps outside the room and she breathed a sigh of relief as Nate threw the door open and rushed quickly to her side.

"Are you okay?" He shouted as her ears continued to ring from the sound. She nodded and he reached into the black duffel bag he had brought. Her eyes widened as he pulled out a gun. He held it pointing upward as he grasped her hand and pulled her to her feet, motioning her to follow him. She did and they inched along the hallway to the living room where they could hear more voices outside.

They neared the front door and Nate dropped her hand, motioning for her to stay back as he scooted towards the open doorway. He peered out and then waved her over. As she obliged she saw that Agent Brockman was on the ground with his leg bleeding profusely and Agent Sims was applying a towel to the mess. The black suburban now lay burning in front of the house, as billows of smoke rushed into the air from its charred shell.

"Get over here and stay down!" Agent Sims yelled, waving Nate over to him frantically. Nate pushed Olivia to sit on the wooden steps in front of the door and told her not to move as he jogged over to the injured agent. Sims took Nate's free hand and replaced his own with it, pushing down on the towel covering Agent Brockman's bloody leg. Agent Sims got up and whipped his gun out, looking around quickly, his eyes scanning the trees around them. Satisfied that the danger was at least not currently nearby he swiftly approached Olivia. She almost cowered at his towering form, his black eyes churning and his hand at the ready on the weapon in his hand. She was surprised she didn't let out a little yelp as he tossed her a black phone.

He motioned towards the device that she now gripped in trembling hands as his eyes continued to survey the area, "Speed dial number one, tell them we have an agent down and we need an ambulance. Let them know suspect is in the area."

Olivia nodded robotically and dialed, relaying the message to the agent on the other line. She then placed the phone down on the porch and watched as the agent rounded the corner of the house to check the perimeter for threats. As she sat there her head started pounding. He had just stated that the 'suspect was in the area'. The guy, the one who had killed the chief and probably those girls too was here somewhere. And here she was, sitting on the porch of what was supposed to be a safe house and suddenly she felt as helpless as a baby deer.

"Olivia!" Nate's voice broke her out of her stupor and she whipped her head up to where he continuing to apply pressure to Agent Brockman's leg. Agent Sims had not yet returned from around the back of the house.

"Get the fire extinguisher from the kitchen; I think I saw it in the pantry yesterday..." He motioned his head over towards the sparks that were now jumping from the burning vehicle to the dry grass surrounding their shelter and causing small fires to erupt. She nodded and headed back in to the house, leaving the cell phone on the steps in her haste. As she entered the door, she closed it behind her in a feeble attempt to keep the smoke from outside from clogging up the interior. This was hard to do, since there was already plenty of smoke swirling around the kitchen and the front room. She hurried over to the pantry and flung the door open but just as she reached in to grab the red canister a hand clamped down hard over her mouth and she felt something cold and hard pressing painfully into her throat.

"Scream and I will kill your boyfriend and that agent he's hanging out with," a hoarse voice whispered menacingly into her ear. Olivia's heart thudded and she nodded in response, her body paralyzed with fear. Her captor began to tug backwards, dragging her towards the bedroom as she struggled to keep the knife from slicing into her throat. They entered the room and he pointed towards the large window, now splayed open with the draperies that had been hiding them from the outside world laying in a heap on the wooden floor.

"Let's go, and remember, say one word and they die." He tugged her roughly up and over the window sill, keeping the knife to her throat and she felt a twinge of pain as it bit into her sensitive skin. A trickle of wetness slid down her neck and the tears started to form as she realized that she did not have many options here. This was her stalker, the one who killed the chief and the one who was finally going to get the chance to kill her. He had outsmarted them all and she knew this was going to be it. They shimmied over the window sill onto the dirt covered ground in back of the house and Olivia sharply inhaled as she spotted Agent Sims lying nearby on the ground, a pool of blood rapidly expanding around his head, his gun lying near his hand.

"Quickly, keep moving!" The man shoved her forcefully in front of him, pushing the blade into the center of her back and they headed into the depths of the forests. Olivia kept her mouth shut as the branches of the dense trees tugged and scratched at her skin. Her feet stumbled on the uneven ground, catching on rocks and tree limbs and when she slowed down he only pushed the knife deeper into her back. Seeing the federal agent on the ground obviously dead kept her from crying out. No matter what this man had in store for her, she was not about to let him hurt or kill Nate.

They reached a rocky open area, and the man pointed a black gloved finger towards a small waterfall that flowed into a tiny pool. Under ordinary circumstances she would have found this piece of nature beautiful, but knowing this would potentially be her deathbed caused her to shiver in fear.

"Go!" He barked at her, shoving her towards the mouth of the waterfall and finally grabbing her arm roughly and swiveling her around until she somehow ended up in a dark cave behind the falls, her back slamming against a cold, damp wall of rock. The man turned quickly as he stepped in behind her and glanced through the cascading water, searching for any sign that they might have been followed.

Satisfied they were alone, he turned towards her and she saw that he was wearing black from head to toe and his head was covered with a ski cap, small slits cut out in the eyes. She tried to memorize his stature and any features she could, on the slim chance that she might make it out alive. He was tall, about 6'1" and of average build. His hair was covered so she couldn't see what color it was but his eyes...his eyes were black, his pupils dilated, she could see nothing but pure evil staring back at her.

Olivia stumbled back and found herself pressed once again against a wet hard wall as she stared at the person in front of her in fear.

"I have been waiting for you my darling," he told her, advancing a step, "For just the perfect time. You are my finale, you will be my masterpiece."

Her eyes wide with fear, Olivia quickly turned and glanced around the dark cave, but there was no exit behind her. He laughed tauntingly at her as he stepped even closer. Her head spun as she felt his breath on her ear.

"Scream and your throat will be split before you can finish," he whispered. Silent tears leaked from her eyes as she stood there, frozen, staring into a blockade of rocks in front of her. Without warning her hair was yanked back and he shoved her down onto the rocky floor, scraping her knee through the thin denim of her jeans.

Olivia wanted to throw up as he pushed her onto her back to straddle her and she thrashed against him in desperation.

He violently grabbed her wrists together in his hand and pushed them over her head. She cried out and shook her head as the tears betrayed her and flowed freely down her face. He slid the knife from her neck down the middle of her chest.

"It's just you and me baby, and I've been waiting for this day for a long time." He told her as he pushed the tip of the knife into the material of her shirt. She sobbed and pleaded with him as she wept.

He threw the knife to the side and wrapped the collar of her shirt into his fist pulling her up to his face until she was staring into the depths of his evil cold blue eyes.

"You were supposed to be different you little bitch. I saw you that day, my angel in the flames and I knew you were special. And then I saw you with *him*, always with him. I could see the desire in both of you when you were around each other. All of you are the same, sluts who care more about getting laid than being decent to other people."

Anger welled up in Olivia and on impulse she spit in his face. He hand continued to grip her top but he froze, startled at her sudden show of defiance. His eyes churned suddenly with dark fury and he reared his hand back and slapped her, hard. She felt the burn on her cheek as her head whipped to the side and knew that he had bruised her.

She cried out as he moved swiftly, pinning her to the ground and pummeling her in the side with his fists.

Quickly and without warning, his weight was off of her and the assault had stopped. She looked up startled to see him flying against the rocky wall of the cave and Nate, standing there; fists clenched and eyes spitting fire. He stood there, hair mussed, clothes torn and Olivia wanted to throw herself around him in relief.

"You son of a bitch!" Nate screamed, charging the masked man and pummeling him into the wall again. He kicked at him and hit him until it looked as though he had lost consciousness.

Satisfied that he had indeed knocked her captor out, Nate took a few deep calming breaths and he hurried over to Olivia as she struggled to sit up, pulling her shirt back down. Nate grabbed her shoulders and looked her over, running his hand along her bruised cheek.

"I'm okay," she whispered, "he was going to kill you. I think he killed Sims."

She threw her arms around him and he rubbed her back in comfort.

"I am so sorry baby; I never should have sent you back into that house. When you didn't come back, I tied my belt around Agent Brockman's leg and left him there to find you. I looked everywhere and then I saw the window, and Sims on the ground. I just ran."

Olivia pulled back to look up at him and her heart broke as she saw the tears welling in his eyes, "How did you find us?"

"The guy was dumb enough to leave the trail of broken tree branches in his wake when he was pulling you along. He was in such a hurry to get to his little hiding spot he didn't think to cover his tracks."

Olivia nodded but before she could say anything else a glint of silver flashed behind Nate and she screamed.

"Look out!" She cried in warning as the man in the mask had gotten to his feet and started to plunge the knife towards his back. Nate pushed her out of the way and whipped around, the knife narrowly missing him. She rolled to the side as the two men wrestled each other and she could see the silver blade in glances as they fought.

He was under Nate now, the blade pointed at Nate's chest and both men gripping its handle. With a jerk, their arms moved and Nate collapsed on top of him, a red liquid oozing from between the both of them. Olivia rushed over and pulled Nate up, as the man lay there, the handle protruding from the wound in his chest, his mask now lifted up and twisted around the top of his head. His face was distorted with burn scars marring his forehead and cheeks. As she watched him, repulsed, his eyes slowly glazed over and finally his breathing stopped and his skin began to pale.

Olivia clung to Nate as he stared down at the man, his face damp with sweat. He wrapped an arm around her and she sobbed as they headed out of the cave and into the open air.

CHAPTER 14

"Are you ready for this?" Nate asked Olivia as she tugged on her Station 61 top and some jeans. She turned to him, admiring his ripped chest and arms in his own black t-shirt and blushed when his green eyes sparkled knowingly.

"Ready as I will ever be..." It had been three weeks since a deranged serial killer with a history of arson due to a childhood abusive trauma had tried to kill her and today was the day of the annual Fourth of July Parade. Olivia was both excited and sad as a part of the parade was to honor Chief Turner. The fire truck had even been decorated with his helmet number and his picture was to be placed at the front of the red engine on a plaque that would eventually be moved in memoriam to the station.

The lieutenant had been officially promoted and Olivia and Nate had been working a lot in the prior weeks with all of the rain that was still coming in from the north. Her apartment had been cleaned and her dining room table was disposed of but she had spent many nights at Nate's apartment since she still had a hard time sleeping at her own place.

The feds had told Olivia that after the incident that they had found locks of hair in his one-bedroom apartment they searched in south Austin. Hair that matched the girls that had been killed and burned in those fires. He had succeeded in murdering a federal agent, a fire chief, and innocent women, but fortunately Agent Brockman and Olivia had survived his rampage. The tourniquet Nate had made with his belt had stopped the bleeding enough for help to arrive. Upon investigation and removal of the killer's body, federal authorities had found explosives slightly deeper in the cave and they believed that the man intended to go out with Olivia in a blaze of glory as his mental break had reached its peak.

Since that day, she had nightmares a few times a week but they were becoming few and far between. She had thrown herself into work and thanks to Anne, had several girl-fests at various spas and salons to relieve her of the stress of what had happened. Today however was supposed to be a perfect day and the whole town was ready to celebrate...and remember.

Nate kissed Olivia deeply and they headed out in his car to meet the guys at the station. They really hadn't seen each other too much outside of work since the incident, but she knew they would have more time off together once the weather changed.

"There is my tough girl," Her father stated

lovingly as she and Nate approached Station 61. He walked over with a smile and threw an arm around her, "Ready for this sweetie?"

Olivia threw her arms up into the air, "Why does everyone keep asking me that?"

Nate and her father laughed at her and she rolled her eyes in response as they walked over to join the rest of the guys near the fire truck.

The emotions around the fire station were somber, with everyone acknowledging that this parade was also a farewell to the Chief. He had no family, his ex-wife was out of the picture, no kids, and even with as mean as the man had been, the firefighters of Station 61 were his family and they felt it their duty to honor his passing in such a way.

They gave the fire truck one last rub down with polishing rags and then everyone climbed on board, and headed to the start of the parade. Nate held Olivia's hand as he sat across from her and they smiled and waved to the families sitting and cheering on the sides of the street. Her father sat beside her and he held her other hand as well. She was surrounded by two men she cared about at one of her favorite events of the year and her spirits were lifted. It was a great turnout, with most of the town in attendance, and Fire Station 61 felt a lift in mood as kids looked up at them in admiration.

"I would say that it's cuz of the chicks," Erik said, waving to a little girl in a wheelchair, "But man, this job really is great because of all the people we help."

Dylan kicked at him, "It's *really* because of the chicks though."

Nate laughed as the rest of the firefighters joined in the banter and Olivia just rolled her eyes and smiled in contentment.

She continued to smile and wave at the passing faces.

"Where's Darcy?" she asked her father after searching the crowd and realizing that the woman was not in their midst.

"Getting the bar ready for the after party of course!" He laughed then sobered quickly as he continued, "Takes a little bit longer these days with her arm in a sling but she should be getting it removed soon and I know she'll be happy about that."

They continued waving and smiling until Olivia's arm grew tired and her cheeks hurt.

The parade finally ended and a special memorial to Chief Turner was given at the end of the route by the lieutenant. It was really very nice as it highlighted his achievements as well as the achievements of Station 61 under his leadership. Despite his abrasive attitude, he had done a fine job of leading a successful fire station.

After the memorial, her father told her he was heading over to see Darcy at the bar and Olivia promised him she would stop by before heading back to the station to shed their gear. The guys not on shift would of course, be able to enjoy the after party at the Corner Bar and it was bound to be a wild time after recent events.

She, Nate and the rest of the guys spent the next twenty minutes shaking hands with the townspeople as they milled about and letting excited children climb all over the fire engine.

"I feel like I'm hugging a celebrity!" Anne exclaimed as she popped up from the crowd and wrapped her arms around Olivia. Olivia rolled her eyes in response but hugged her friend back eagerly, glad that things were starting to feel as if they were getting back to normal.

"Hey blondie, my, my, my, don't we look utterly adorable today," Erik teased as he sidled up next to Anne and gave her a not-so-subtle once over.

"Not as adorable as you looked waving to the kiddies in your little red fire truck," Anne retorted with a coy smile, "I'm surprised your helmet fits over that big head of yours."

Erik seemed taken aback for a second and then he grinned, a dimple forming in his cheek. He threw an arm around Anne and steered her towards the parking lot.

"Well now that that's out of the way, let me buy you dinner," he told her as he guided her towards his car. Anne looked up at him in a flash of surprise and her cheeks flushed as she threw a questioning glance Olivia's way. Nodding encouragingly at her friend, Olivia gave Anne a wave and then shook her head and smiled as the two sauntered off.

"Never saw that one coming," Dylan muttered as he stared slack-jawed after Erik and Anne in disbelief.

Nate looked curiously at Olivia and she just shrugged and chuckled, shaking her head.

After some more meet and greets, the crowd finally began to thin out and Olivia turned towards Nate.

"I'm going to pop in and say a quick goodbye to Dad and Darcy before we head back for our shift."

"Don't be long," he replied as he kissed her on the cheek, earning a groan from Erik. Olivia laughed and responded to Erik's eye roll with a flirty wave as she headed up the street to the old brick building that housed Darcy's bar. As she got closer she saw that the "Open" sign was not yet turned on, which was strange because she knew Darcy would have had the bar ready to go as soon as the parade was over.

Figuring someone had just forgotten to flip on the sign, she approached the bar and yanked on the door handles, surprised to find that they weren't budging. She gave the door a sharp rap and glanced around to watch the few straggling parade goers walking off or climbing into vehicles on the nearby streets as they headed home. Some of them glanced at the bar but seeing that the sign was off turned and walked the other way. Olivia stood and waited for a few short moments and then knocked again, louder this time. When she still didn't get an answer, Olivia peered into the windows of the bar and glanced around at the bar stools that were already set up for the day. She was just about to get out her phone to call her father when she spotted what looked like a person tied up in a chair behind the bar, barely visible through the foggy glass.

"Dad! Darcy!" She called out, frantically yanking on the locked doors. They wouldn't give and she knew the only other way into the building was the door around back. They always kept those unlocked to throw out trash during the day and for the employees to come in and out when they wanted a smoke. Olivia dashed around the side of the building to the back door but when she reached the handle a blinding pain seared through her head and everything went black.

CHAPTER 15

Olivia's eyes felt heavy and her lashes seemed almost fused together as she struggled to open them. Something was causing her vision to remain dark, and although she could see particles of light, whatever device had been placed over her eyes obscured her sight almost entirely. Her head throbbed and she was curled up in a roped cattle position, her hands bound together by something (tape?) and her feet as well (rope?). What felt like duct tape had been placed tightly over her mouth and she struggled to breathe through her nose. She strained to listen and could make out the sound of cars, wind, and light music. And then she realized where she was.

I'm inside of a trunk, she thought with horror. *But the killer is dead, who could this person be?* A million thoughts started running through her head. Had they really gotten the killer? Were there two killers? Was Nate worried about her? What had happened to her father? To Darcy? Oh God, what if they were dead? She struggled to contain the vomit that threatened to rise from her throat into her currently plastered shut mouth.

Olivia thrust her hands forward and felt around desperately in the darkness of the small space. *Maybe there is a trunk release somewhere*, she thought. Okay so perhaps that was a stretch but she could not think of anything else to try. As her bound hands groped the carpeted, almost sticky flooring of the trunk, her fingertips felt nothing but empty space. She jumped slightly as someone suddenly coughed. *A woman?* Olivia thought. She heard someone mumble. There were two of them! A man and a woman. What the hell was going on?

The road abruptly became uneven and the ache at the back of her head worsened with every bump the vehicle hit. Before she could even begin to wonder where they were taking her she realized that the car had stopped. Her heart thudded loudly in her chest as she painfully waited to see what would happen to her next. More mumbling could be heard and then the sound of car doors slamming as heavy, approaching footsteps crunched on gravel.

Olivia lay there quietly, frightened out of her mind, praying that if they were going to kill her that they would get it over with quickly. She heard a key enter the trunk lock and for a moment she stopped breathing, frozen with fear as she heard the squeal of metal lifting and a breeze blow over her cheeks.

"Is she dead?" Someone, the woman, asked almost sarcastically.

Olivia felt heavy hands suddenly grasp and

shake her shoulders violently, causing the pain in her head to worsen and she uttered out a strangled cry behind the gag.

"Nah, she's just playing dead, dumb bitch must think we're stupid." The male voice said with a huff. The hands that had been shaking Olivia gripped her arms roughly and pulled her out of the trunk. She winced and tears welled in my eyes as her body scraped the edge of the car trunk and then the ground as he roughly dragged her out and deposited her on the floor. Tiny rocks burned into the fresh scrapes on her skin and from her position on the ground she could smell stale cigarette butts nearby.

Olivia was picked up and heaved over a big shoulder and her head and body screamed in pain as she was toted along carelessly. Her arms dangled down his back and she made feeble attempts to yank her bound wrists apart as she bounced along. No sooner had she attempted to weaken the tape that held her hands together, was she then tossed painfully to the ground again, this time, thankfully, landing on grass. She heard something heavy being opened, more creaking metal. Another trunk maybe? A van?

"I ain't carrying her down there," the man said gruffly.

The woman laughed cruelly and Olivia sobbed into her gag as a foot stomped into her back and she fell, tumbling down some steps and landing with a thud on hard concrete, her head slamming into the floor as stars flashed through her eyelids. She tugged frantically at her restraints as footsteps descended what must have been a stairwell and neared her.

"Okay bitch, I'm going to untie you but you better not scream, run, or look at me or I'll slit your throat right here, got it?" The voice of the cruel woman cut through Olivia like a knife with the promise behind it.

She nodded weakly and the tape was viciously ripped off her eyes and mouth, bringing more tears to her eyes as she blinked rapidly in an attempt to adjust to a bright light that was streaming down at her. After the kidnapper had removed the restraints at her hands and feet she cowered in place, afraid to move.

Olivia tried to look up at the person standing in front of her and a fist flew at her cheek, knocking her backwards into the wall.

"I said not to fucking look at me you stupid bitch!" Olivia trembled and averted her face as the female walked over to her. She flinched as something sharp touched the side of her neck and with her cheek now throbbing she attempted to keep her gaze down towards her feet, which she just realized were bare and scraped up the ankles from the rough transport.

"Don't worry about it," The man's voice carried down the stairwell loudly, "Let the boss deal with her, she'll be begging for you to come back after he takes care of her."

Both of them laughed maniacally and the angry tip of the blade nicked Olivia's neck in warning as the woman pushed it threateningly into her skin and then removed it, laughing as they left her in her cowering position.

Olivia hugged her arms to her aching body and stayed huddled against the wall as she heard them leave and the heavy metal door coming down loudly with a bang and what sounded like a heavy latch. She listened to make sure she could not hear them anymore and then she took in her surroundings.

She was in a cave, or maybe a shelter of some sort. There were steps leading up to a door in the ceiling and the room contained nothing but a concrete floor, a potato sack and a small lamp in the corner. The smell of bleach permeated the air and a bucket sat near the lamp. Olivia cringed as she realized what that was intended to be used for.

How long am I going to be down here? She thought fearfully as she slowly got to her feet, stumbling as she tried to regain her balance and rubbing her now bruised cheek and the bump on the back of her head. Carefully, Olivia climbed the stairs slowly, her legs screaming at her with every step, and pushed hard on the latch of the door. Of course it was locked.

She looked around the room but all she could see were dirt walls and a concrete floor save for a small vent in the middle of the room. She sat down on the potato sack and examined the damage to her body. Other than her bruise and bump on her face and head, she had only minor scrapes up the side of her body from being dragged and the small scrapes of her feet. Remembering about her phone, she reached into her back pocket but her stomach dropped when she came up empty. Of course, the kidnappers would have taken her phone. Or did she drop it when she was taken? She couldn't remember anything after the sharp pain that had apparently been a syringe had hit her neck outside of the bar.

She thought of her father. Was he alright? Was he killed after he was used as bait? What about Darcy? Who could have done this? The killer was already dead. She saw his body, she *knew* he was dead. He had admitted to the killings and the fires right in front of her. So why were these people after her? And who was the guy they were talking about earlier that would be coming to hurt her?

Olivia thought of Nate. *He'll find me*, she assured herself, *He'll keep looking, I know he will.* He would check the bar for Olivia, find her father and Darcy and then come looking for her. Gorgeous eyes and dimples flew through her brain and for the first time she didn't hold back the tears that fell. She cried because for the first time, she realized that she could not live without Nate. He was her everything and she wanted to love him forever but now might not ever get the chance to tell him.

She rolled the musty potato sack up and

gently laid her head down on it as the tears fell and she drifted into a painful, fitful sleep.

CHAPTER 16

Olivia awoke in confusion, her neck aching from sleeping on the hard ground and realized that someone was standing over her. She scrambled back on all fours quickly, pressing up hard against the wall and rapidly blinking sleep from her eyes.

As her vision cleared and adjusted to the light streaming in from the now-open door at the top of the stairs she focused on the figure in front of her and her jaw dropped in disbelief.

"Seeing ghosts are we *Miles*?" Chief Turner's voice dripped with disdain as he stood before her with bloodshot eyes, "after all this time, you are here with me now and you will pay for what you have done."

Her voice trembled as she tried to open her mouth to speak but only syllables came out, "What, How?"

He laughed louder, "Always the innocent little victim. Well I know better. You all are the same. Expect men to bend over backwards for you, take what you want then leave us out to dry. You did the same with your father."

"What?" Olivia was perplexed and still in

shock, "You were dead, I saw..."

Turner paced in front of her, chuckling to himself and cracking his large knuckles roughly.

"What you saw was some hair from my head, some of my blood, but everything else was... let's say, 'borrowed' from an old friend of mine."

Olivia wanted to vomit.

"Lucky for me, the police tested enough blood to prove it was my blood type but I knew it would take them time to sort through the other body parts and eventually find out they had not necessarily come from me."

He turned suddenly then reached down and grabbed the collar of her shirt, yanking her roughly to him. The smell of cigarettes and liquor permeated her nostrils and it took all she had to not hurl on him at that very moment.

His eyes burned into hers as he spoke, "Time to finally take care of the pain that has been in my ass for years."

She turned her head quickly away, wincing as she attempted to struggle away from the odor and craziness that was oozing from the chief.

He released her shirt as she pulled back, causing her to bounce painfully against the wall, her head knocking against the hard surface again and irritating the bump that was still there from earlier. Olivia stared up at him in horror and disbelief.

"You hate me so much that you would fake your death and then kill me?" She shouted, almost angrily now at the audacity of it all.

His eyes darkened again and he glared at her, "That was not part of the plan originally. I had a partner, someone who was going to finish the job. Someone who was part of the plan all along. But he turned out to be nothing but a big disappointment."

Her eyes widened in shock, "The arsonist? The killer? He was your partner?"

"Well, not initially," the chief shrugged as he carelessly rubbed the stubble on his large chin and began pacing again. "I approached him after the first fire, the one when they found the body. You see, I saw him in the trees that day, I saw him watching you from the darkness while I waited for you and the others by the truck. And I saw the hunger in his eyes. I knew I would be able to use him. Use his new obsession with you to my advantage. He saw me that day too. And he saw the understanding in my eyes, saw me nod at him in silent contract and understanding. After that we met in secret, rolling out our plans."

He laughed, "Of course, I never told him that I wanted to kill you. I simply played the role of the understanding associate. The one who appreciated his work with arson and fire and who pushed him towards you. I knew that in the end you would do something to betray his image of you and like a typical woman you in fact proved me right in the end."

She cowered as he lunged at her, gripping

her hair tightly in his hands and yanking her face up to meet his. She whimpered in pain as he leaned in close.

"All he had to do was see you and your little hero boyfriend together once and he was done. His image of you was shattered and he was ready to destroy you. Unfortunately for him I figured it would not end well as he got sloppy with his obsession for you. So I staged my death knowing that I would need a Plan B to finally get rid of you."

"You are fucking crazy!" Olivia yelled in anger as her hair felt like it was being ripped from her scalp. "Did you kill my father too?!!"

Turner shook his head as she struggled against the clenched fist that gripped her mane.

"I just needed a distraction, I knew you would be coming to the bar after the parade and I needed you where my hired associates could easily take you. I left him there knowing your *boyfriend* would find him eventually when he came looking for you. Wish I could have seen the looks on their faces when they realized you were gone."

Olivia's blood boiled and she reached up and gripped the wrists that held her in place, swinging her legs forward and catching Turner on the shins hard.

He cursed and released his hold but quickly recovered and backhanded her mouth hard. The taste of metal filled her mouth as she landed on the ground with a groan. Too fatigued to move, Olivia could only scream as he reared back and kicked her in the ribs, hard. An excruciating pain radiated down her side and she knew that he had bruised a rib or two. She howled in pain, clutching her side as he rubbed his shins and spit on the ground near her.

"You stupid bitch," he growled, "I am definitely going to enjoy torturing you before I kill you." With that he turned and stomped heavily up the stairs, slamming the door shut and leaving her in the semi-darkness.

Olivia lifted her hand gingerly to her mouth and pulled it back to examine the blood that now flowed freely from her split lip. Stars danced across her irises as the blinding pain in her ribs tore through her body with every turn. She curled up on her side as she sobbed at the physical and emotional pain that had been inflicted on her. Exhausted, she once again passed out in the semi-darkness.

A creaking sound made her cringe and scrambled up and against the wall as the latch to the door opened. She reached over grabbed the lantern and gripped it tight as sunlight flooded the room yet again. She squinted against the brightness and prepared her body for one last fight.

As strong hands grabbed her by the arms she screamed and swung the lantern upwards, kicking with what little strength she had in her until he let go. Olivia clutched at her side as the pain of her bruised ribs splintered upwards but found the strength to bolt past him and clamber up the concrete steps, his cursing reaching up to meet her.

As she reached the top of the steps she kept running, not taking the time to look behind her and stumbling over the uneven gravel that covered the ground before her. Flashes of fields and what looked like a large open parking lot flew by her vision as she ran but all she could focus on was the canopy of dense trees that stretched out before her.

"Get back here!" A voice bellowed behind her in the distance and Olivia picked up speed, ignoring the sharp pains in her ribs as she tore through the foliage. She zigzagged as she ran, trying to keep him off her trail as the branches scraped at her skin. After running a fair amount, she finally stopped and crouched behind a tree, listening for any signs that Turner was near. Birds chirped and leaves rustled slightly with the breeze but she couldn't hear any indication that he was close by.

She glanced upwards and saw that the tree she was hovering by had some slender but sturdy branches so on a whim Olivia began scaling the tree, taking time to not strain her ribs too much as she climbed higher and higher into the dense leaves. Finally she reached what seemed like a good hiding spot and so she sat and waited, trying not to move in order to keep herself hidden. What seemed like ages passed as she sat there and waited, pressing her back against the bark and keeping her legs wrapped securely around the branch below her. She held her breath as she heard the clambering of footsteps looming closer. The sun was now receding and she could hardly see through the darkness that was fast approaching.

"Come out, come out wherever you are!" Turner taunted as she heard him brushing aside branches and scouring the area for any signs of her. She tried to breathe slowly and quietly, but her ribs were now burning with pain and her backside was rapidly becoming numb as she sat on the uncomfortable limb. She shifted slightly and a branch snapped under her foot. Olivia froze, her breathing stopped altogether as she could hear the chief's steps turning towards the tree she was hiding in. She waited and listened, knowing that he was probably straining to see through the thick leaves to find her. She held her position as the sun fell deeper into the distance and the darkness turned to utter black, the moonlight glancing off of the waxy green of the foliage.

Finally Olivia heard Turner continue walking, hacking away at branches with some kind of weapon and cursing as he called out her name. She stayed still and listened to his footsteps receding deeper into the forest and when she had no longer heard him for several minutes she carefully crept back down the branches and landed silently on the forest floor. It was almost pitch black now and she prayed that she was heading the right way when she started to walk quietly away from the direction she had heard him heading. She kept close to tree branches, stopping every so often to listen for signs that he might had heard her and was coming close.

Olivia walked and followed the trail that Turner had left on his way into the forest, the broken branches and scattered leaves leading a path back out to the open where she would hopefully find a road she could follow to civilization. A sudden *snap* from behind her caused her to swivel around quickly, and a sharp gasp emitted from her throat as a startled raccoon raised its widened eyes at her and then scampered off into the forest.

She blew out a breath and turned back around only to slam right into Turner's chest. Olivia lost her balance and fell backwards, hitting her elbow on a rock in the process and sending a shooting pain through her arm. Turner smiled down at her, teeth glistening like the fangs of a predator as he held an ax over his shoulder, bits of leaves and branch residue clinging to the sharp blade.

"Tsk tsk little girl," he goaded her; "You really think after all this time I would just let you get away?"

Olivia cringed as he swung the ax down but he stopped short of striking her with it and the blade buried sharply into the ground beside her head. Turner leaned down and yanked her up by her hair, tugging her onto her feet and sending sears of pain once again through her scalp. She struggled to her feet and the chief swung his arm around, throwing her towards a nearby tree and smiling triumphantly as she struck the base of the trunk and collapsed into a heap. She lay there gasping for breath as she heard him pick up the ax again.

She heard the rush of the air as he swung his ax and on impulse she rolled to the right, relieved when she heard the metal connect with the tree. She heard him curse and stomp towards her and she reached down and gripped the dirt with both hands.

The sound of his shouts satisfied her as she flung the dirt into his eyes, temporarily blinding him and she dashed away quickly as he stood there, clawing at his burning eyes and yelling after her.

She flew through the trees, ignoring the branches that slapped at her arms and face as she ran. She neared the clearing but as she got closer, her foot caught on an upturned root and she cried out as she flew roughly to the ground, her knee banging a rock and shooting pain through her leg.

Tears of pain leaked from her eyes as she held her knee and struggled to get up. She flipped onto her back and gasped as she saw Turner advancing on her.

"No more games," he said menacingly and she shut her eyes and held up her arms in weak defense as she heard the rush of the wind slicing through the swinging blade. She waited for the sting of metal to cut her delicate flesh but nothing came. As she looked up she realized that the chief was no longer in front of her but several feet away, the ax laying near him on the ground and two agents struggling to cuff him.

"Is she okay? Where is she?!!"

The voice brought tears to her eyes and she squinted into the dark, the flashlights held by several more agents entering the area bouncing off the trees as they came closer. A concerned Nate came barreling in between two agents and the tears flowed down her cheeks as he approached her.

"Are you real?" She asked as he knelt crouched over her, looking as if he was afraid to touch her. She heard the agents scuffling with Turner and heard him shouting and cursing in anger.

"I'm real baby," Nate responded, tears welling in his beautiful green eyes. "Are you hurt, can you stand?"

In response she flew into his arms and clutched at his shirt, sobbing into it.

"It's okay," he told her, rubbing her back gently, "He can't hurt you anymore."

She peeked under his arm at Turner who was now being led away in handcuffs through the forest, a bitter scowl on his face, and fury flying from his eyes into hers. A female agent nearby came over and helped them to their feet.

"Miss, do you have any injuries?" The brunette petite woman asked her gently.

"I think my ribs are bruised, maybe broken, and I hit my head a few times in that basement, among other things."

Nate sucked in an angry breath and Olivia looked up at him.

"How did you all find me?" She asked.

"Your cell phone must have slipped out of your pocket because Detective Gray was able to track it to the trunk of those assholes that kidnapped you. Somehow it had slipped under the trunk liner onto the wheel well and those idiots didn't think to search you when they grabbed you. When they got pulled over they admitted to taking you but told the cops that Turner was the one who arranged it and they were only in it for the money. Then they led us here. We heard the commotion and were able to rush over here to find you."

Nate and the female agent flanked her carefully on both sides and supported her weight as she stumbled on the grass and uneven ground. Once they reached the edge of the gravel lot, Olivia saw several black vehicles and an ambulance with flashing lights had pulled up near the open metal door that led to her temporary prison.

"We've got to get you to a doctor, okay?" Nate told Olivia and she nodded tearfully as he gently picked her up and carried her to the waiting ambulance. He jumped quickly into the back with her and the ambulance took off, speeding and blaring sirens all the way to the hospital. They admitted her to a room and she was hooked up to an IV with fluids as the doctor did his inspection.

* * *

Olivia woke to a faint buzzing noise and a dim room. Glancing over, she saw that her IV had been removed and that the noise she was hearing was coming from the monitor she was hooked up to. *How long have I been out?* She thought.

The end of the bed felt heavy and she carefully leaned up to see Nate sitting in a chair at the foot of the bed, his arms draped over her legs and his head resting on the edge of the bed. She took in the tousled hair, the shadow on his face, the dark circles under his eyes and she felt a twinge of pain along with adoration.

His eyes slowly opened and as he realized that she was awake he lifted his head up, "Hey," he smiled, stretching his arms out and yawning. He scooted his chair up the bed and leaned over to kiss her forehead. "How are you feeling?"

"Tired," she admitted, "How long have I been out?"

"Two days," he said, interlacing his fingers with hers.

Her breath caught. "Two days?" Olivia sat up quickly, only to have Nate lean her back down as stars dotted he vision.

"Easy there, you're still recovering," he scolded.

"Sweetheart?"

Olivia turned towards the hospital room door and a wave of relief fell over her as her father rushed towards her, a bouquet of flowers in his hand, tears welling in his tired old eyes. He rushed to her and swept her into a gentle hug, leaning over her hospital bed and almost causing Nate to fall onto the floor in the process.

"I'm okay dad, really," she assured him as she squeezed her arms around him.

Her father pulled back and kissed her on the forehead, and then he looked into her eyes with love. She smiled at him and Darcy who had joined him and had brought her own bouquet of flowers, beautiful white lilies. Olivia thanked them as they placed the flowers next to her bedside and Nate motioned for Darcy to sit in his chair as he moved to lean against the hospital window.

"What's going to happen to Turner?" Olivia asked as she self-consciously smoothed her hair back into its low ponytail. Her father glanced at Nate quickly and then nodded and her eyes narrowed.

"What's up?" She asked them accusingly.

"Turner's dead hon," her father told her, not sounding too sorry about it, "He hanged himself in his cell a few hours after the Feds caught him. He was going to be put on trial for attempted murder and murder. They found out the, well, organs he borrowed for his little setup at your apartment was his ex-wife's. Guess he figured he had no leg to stand on if he went to trial."

Olivia considered that for a moment as emotions such as relief, sadness, confusion, and anger ran through her. Her father and Nate looked at her expectantly and, not wanting to concern them, she shrugged.

"At least I won't have to testify in court or anything," she concluded, not sure how she felt about Turner taking his own life instead of spending the rest of eternity in a dank little cell. But she knew that meant that she could live her life, not worrying about him ever getting out of prison and hurting her or anyone else again.

"That's my girl," Nate chuckled as he ruffled the ponytail she had just tried to smooth out, "Always the optimist."

"The doctor says you'll be good to go tomorrow sweetie," her father told her, "Unfortunately you'll have to recount what happened to the Feds before you get released."

Darcy quickly added, "After that we can take you back to your apartment to let you get some rest."

"I'm thinking about moving anyway," Olivia replied wearily with a sigh. She just couldn't stay in that apartment any longer. Any time she looked at the kitchen counter she knew she would see body parts and blood.

Nate scratched at his stubble, "Well, I was hoping maybe, that you'd want to stay with me." He glanced at her nervously; fidgeting with the cords on the window blinds, then stole a look at her father, his cheeks reddening. Her father simply smiled and folded his arms, watching the both of them in amusement.

The butterflies in her stomach picked up speed, "For how long?" She managed to squeak out. She wrung her hands on the sheets hopefully as she watched him anxiously. Her father and Darcy, she noticed, had gotten up and were slipping quietly out of the room.

He shrugged nonchalantly then peered intensely into her eyes, "I love you Liv, and you know that. I want you to stay with me all the time. I want to wake up next to you, I want to work with you, and I want to spend as many seconds of the day with you as possible. I almost lost you and I'm not going to waste any more of my life without you."

"I'd like that," She blew out the breath she had been holding and smiled. He leaned in and kissed her gently on the mouth and she fell back into a blissful sleep.

EPILOGUE

A month later, Olivia's ribs were healed and she was back on her feet again and ready to get back to work. She had spent the past weeks recuperating, with daily visits from her dad and Darcy and of course Anne and Erik, who were now spending more time together as a couple to the dismay of the female firehouse visitors. Nate and her father had moved her things out of her apartment and into Nate's house and she was starting to feel very comfortable there. The nights she had trouble sleeping she would sit out on the porch with a cup of tea and just watch the stars. The nightmares were receding as Nate said they would and it helped that he was there on the nights he was off to comfort her.

She was making coffee when Nate called. He had been on shift already and she was going to be going in for her first day back shortly. Unfortunately he was calling to let her know that they were being called out to a fire and she would have to drive herself instead of him being able to swing by and pick her up. Olivia didn't mind. She was happy to get back into the swing of things and knew it would be the final step she needed to get her entire life back.

The killer Turner had been working with, a young man with a troubled childhood named Hugh Chester, had been killed in the scuffle with Nate; however since he had blown up a federal agent, that case was closed just as quickly as it was opened. For the first time in a long time, Olivia finally felt safe.

Soon after the story had leaked about the chief and Olivia's involvement with the serial killer arsonist, reporters had begun flooding the fire station and Nate's home and they had to continuously fight them off. To appease them, Detective Gray suggested that Olivia give one public interview about the ordeal and she did, addressing everyone all at once in a news conference in Austin. Fortunately the detective had been right and the satisfied reporters had eventually dwindled until hardly any lurked about.

Olivia shook herself out of her thoughts as she pulled up to the parking lot at the station and was surprised to see the fire truck was already back from its outing.

Must have been a small fire, she thought as she grabbed her bag and started to head into the 61. She inhaled deeply as she took her first step into the garage and her foot crunched down on something. She looked down and spotted a white rose which she gingerly picked up, avoiding the pointed tips of the thorns. Looking even further into the garage in confusion, Olivia saw a slew of white roses had been thrown about and led in a path deeper into Station 61. She picked each one up as she walked, her heart pounding curiously.

As she rounded the corner, Nate stood there wearing a tailored black suit and holding a dozen red roses. Her father, Darcy, Erik, Anne, Dylan, Scott, Matt and the lieutenant stood next to him beaming.

"This is one heck of a welcome back party," Olivia stated as she took the bouquet that Nate handed to her and he gave her a swift kiss on the cheek.

"This is more than a welcome back party sweetheart," Nate declared as he grasped her hand and lowered himself down onto one knee.

To my amazing husband, my best friend, my life partner. This book would not be what it is today without your faith and encouragement. Thank you for always pushing me towards my fullest potential.